Marilyn Pavlovsky

HONORABLE LIFE

HONORABLE LIFE

Is Published by: The Author

Other Titles
By this Author
are
BURNING SUNSHINE
(2008)
&

THE REVEREND'S DAUGHTER
(2010)

HONORABLE LIFE
Copyright © 2009 by Marilyn Pavlovsky
Rights Owner: Marilyn Pavlovsky
Publisher: Marilyn Pavlovsky
Language: English
Country: United States
Edited by: WRGA Edit - S. Short, Editor
Edition: First Edition
Version: 8
Storefront: ID:6037787 LuLu Publishing, Inc.
Websites   www.book-burningsunshine.com

Library of Congress Control Number: 2010903553

ISBN 978-0-615-29628-9

Dedication

I dedicate this book to my parents,
Though Daddy's gone, I give to them,
my love.

" Everyone gathered around the box radio in the corner. They could not believe their ears. Pearl Harbor had just been bombed! "

Chapter 1

In the late 1930's and the early 1940's, there were hopeful times around farm areas in the United States. The problems caused by the great depression were subsiding. Many people felt they could start living normal lives once again. Germany had invaded Poland, causing a declaration of war in September 1939. Everyone realized that Germany was a country to be reckoned with. There was no doubt about that. It looked as if there was going to be conflict for the rest of the world with Germany from every angle. There were rumbles all over the world. As for the United States, they were just happy to be coming out of the horrible depression.

A young man named James George Dahl lived on a relatively small farm of about two-hundred-sixty acres, give or take a few acres. This farm was located in Gallia County, Ohio. James lived with his mother, a brother and two sisters. The family was made up of nine children but most had left home by this date to pursue their life's dreams. It was very common in the young man's community for people to get their education; then move to the city of Columbus, Ohio. This city was about one-hundred miles away from the Dahl farm.

The Dahl farm was located in what people called the rolling hills of Ohio. There was a reason for the massive migration of the young people. There was absolutely no industry in the pretty farm land. Mrs. Dahl had once worked in Columbus, Ohio. One of James's sisters, who had died at a very early age, had lived and worked in Columbus, Ohio. Some of James's other siblings were either there or had already planned to move to this city. James was sure it was just a matter of time before they would all leave the farm. He, on the other hand was just as determined to make his living and his life on the farm. Being the youngest son, James knew even if his desires had been different he could not leave his mother on the farm to fend for herself.

James was a rather tall large built dark headed man. Everyone was forever telling him of how very handsome he was. He had shoulders as wide as a barn. When people would joke with him about his size or his looks he would just laugh and agree with them. His sense of humor was large and great in every way. His mother had told him he was born big. She told him that he had all of those muscles from the very day he was born, but he believed it was more from the hard work one does on a farm.

There had been a lot of sadness in the Dahl family while James was just a boy. His father had died when he was only ten. Shortly thereafter he lost an older sister to tuberculosis. Within a year he had lost his oldest brother to a ruptured stomach ulcer. This young man had seen much grief from the death of many loved ones. He had somehow dealt with it all, and had somewhere along the line, became a very jolly, happy person. He loved to tease everyone. Being the youngest son and having two younger sisters, he would often pick on them until his mother would have to stop him. The girls would think it was funny to a point, but they would get mad at him after awhile.

James had a brother named Dale Henderson. He called him Duke. Duke was to marry shortly and leave the farm the same as the others. In Columbus, Ohio this brother would go to work on a job and finish his education. James and this brother were the only two sons who had not finished their schooling. The Dahl family had planned none of this. Their parents once had big plans for all of their children and had saved well for their futures. Money became slim after the deaths of Mr. Dahl, then the eldest son and the daughter. Top that off by a depression in the United States. All of these things had caused much turmoil in the Dahl household. This caused there to be nothing left for Mrs. Dahl to do but to pull James and Dale out of school, permanently.

Mrs. Dahl had taken each one of the two youngest sons out of classes periodically to help work on the farm. Eventually, she had to remove them from school altogether. Their brother Everett had been the only man left to tend to the farm after the untimely death of their elder brother. Everett was married and had a family of his own. He lived in an old log cabin on the lower part of the farm. Their mother had tried very hard to teach her younger sons during the evening hours. She did this by oil lamps. She did the very best she could, but felt she came up short. Both James and Dale knew they must finish their schooling at some future date.

Dale now had a position in Columbus, Ohio. He would, however, get the rest of his education by joining the United States Military. He planned to be in the National Guard. This would give him the training he would need, while allowing him to work a job at home and be with his new bride. He would only have to go to his training a few weeks at a time. The government would then pay for him a higher education. James, on the other hand, had not put much thought into when or how he was going to finish his schooling. Mother had always insisted each child do that very thing.

Mrs. Dahl was highly educated for a lady of her times. She was born in 1883. She had been a nurse. Their mother had been raised near the city of New Orleans, Louisiana. She was raised on a plantation. Tragedy seemed to follow this lovely lady around. She had lost her parents when she was a teen. This had forced her and her siblings to move to the Ohio Valley to live with relatives.

Mrs. Dahl came from a more privileged world. She came from a world where young ladies had received a higher education even during the nineteenth century. Much poorer class of people would only educate their young men.

Over the years, Mrs. Dahl had changed many of her ideas and beliefs. However, she had held tightly onto her belief in the need of a higher education. She also believed very strongly in the equality of men and women. She believed that young men and young women alike must have the very best of education. There was one lucky break for the Dahl family members. That break was whoever wished to learn had every chance in the world to do so. The family owned many books due to the fact that in those times it was required that the families purchase school books needed for education. Due to the size of the Dahl family, there were many, many books. A lot of them may have been worn, but were useable just the same.

James was a very smart young man and he loved to study. He excelled in math with the greatest of ease in all mathematical areas. His mother would often tease him by saying,

"I watch your face as you are calculating something. I expect you to stick out your tongue and at any minute a tape with numbers on it is going to start rolling out of your mouth".
If anyone had a math question, it was always directed towards James.

Mrs. Dahl had always made each child study every evening. The children's study habits only increased once their eldest sister Elizabeth had become a school teacher. No one could escape the pressures of getting an education, it was unavoidable. It was almost force fed to this family. This was very true no matter how hard one may try to get out of that higher education. Mrs. Dahl and her daughter made higher education mandatory for the family.

Oil lamps were the drawback in night studying. However, this did not detour the Dahl family. They kept collecting books and never, ever refused one that someone would offer them. Relaxation at this farm was always reading a book or the Bible. It was hard to read by oil lamp unless you sat right on top of a lamp. During the summer months James was much too hot blooded for that. Most of his reading was done in midday while taking a twenty or thirty-minute break. However, these breaks were very few and far in between. It was very wise to take these breaks during summer months. The hot sun and the extreme hard farm work could take a toll on a person. This family felt they really did not have the time to take these breaks very often whether they needed one or not. So they rarely took one.

Electric was plentiful in all of the cities by this time and had been for many years now. However, rural areas were not on the top of the electric company's list. Often homes were many miles apart. The cost to the electric companies, as well as to the farmers, would be massive. So in this part of the rolling hills of Southern Ohio, hopes of electricity were way out into the future. Unfortunately, the Dahl family would be without power for several more years.

Many people were telling of city life. They told of how people now had inside plumbing and went to the bathroom in the house. James laughed at that thought, as he felt that was surely nasty. His family had a very nice outside toilet that was way out at the end of the chicken house. They kept lye in it and it was quite clean and comfortable.

Friends and family members told of large bath tubs with running water in them. James sure liked that idea. He felt he could really get used to that! That idea sounded very nice. As of now, James would often drive to the little town called Ewington most evenings. This town was about two miles from the farm. The purpose of this trip was for a bath. He would climb into the Raccoon Creek. He would take a bar of soap and a towel. He would get into the shallow part of the water and soap all over. He would then get into the deeper water to rinse off.

James was not that great of a swimmer. However, he knew how to float quite well. Even with that, he could only float while he was on his back. He would often let himself float down the creek a ways and then swim back. He considered his swimming by a term called *dog paddling*. When he may have floated too far down the creek, it took him quite awhile to get back with his lack of knowledge in the swimming department. He would finally make it back to where he had left his towel. This refreshing bath was especially wonderful after one had been working in the hay. You know! The kind of hot and sweaty to where the hay somehow stays stuck upon your skin while it itches all over your body. The creek was a wonderful place to remove this hay and other debris. Dale and Everett loved this way of bathing too. So on hot summer nights these trips to Ewington often became pilgrimages for these young men.

Chapter 2

James Dahl's oldest sister, Elizabeth, taught school in a village called Rutland. This town was several miles over into the next county. Elizabeth had completed her education by attending a local college. She was now married to her High School sweetheart. She and her husband had two adorable children named Simon and Ruth. It was as if James could have been an older brother to Simon. Simon was the first grandchild to the Dahl family. James was only eleven years old when this little lad was born. This made him very close to the child. Simon would sometimes call James (Uncle), but most of the time he would just call him Dutch. Dutch was a name that his brother Dale Henderson had given him years ago. It had stuck on him like glue, the same as Duke had stuck on Dale.

Elizabeth and her husband Matthew had purchased a nice farm. This farm was adorned by a cozy little farm house. It had gingerbread trim all over it. Gingerbread was a term used to describe fancy wood work. James could never figure out how gingerbread could describe such a thing, but none the less, that is what it was called. A porch wrapped around this pretty little home. Big oak trees lined the front lawn. The yard was high above the road and there was a road bank with vines upon it. Elizabeth had planted flowers clear up to the porch. The inside was very pretty as well. After you arrived into the front living room, you could see the dining room straight ahead. Then there were big cabinets with long doors on them. The bottom smaller doors had nothing behind them. They were more for a purpose of a room divider. When these doors were opened you could see straight across the counter and down into a step-down kitchen.

The kitchen had a wood cooking stove and a water pump on top of a counter. The well was directly under this pump. This was unlike the well at the Dahl home where the water had to be carried into the house. The kitchen was ground level and a concrete type floor was used. A drain was in the middle of the floor for overruns that might happen when pumping water. This made the kitchen very cool most of the time. All bedrooms were on the right side of the house, just as if someone had split the house right down the middle. It also had some bedrooms upstairs. James had a big interest in carpentry so he thought this design to be fascinating. He felt that his sister and her family had a very pretty place. A very pretty place indeed!

James had always been very close to this older sister Elizabeth. As a child, she had seemed much more like another mother to him. In the Dahl family the older children looked after the younger children then passed these duties on down to the smallest. James would spend any free time he had with this sister, her husband, niece and nephew. This was partly because he loved to be there and partly because he had complete control of the old Model T anymore. Since his mother's idea of driving was riding side saddle on a horse, or steering a team of horses to pull a buggy, she was not interested in learning how to drive a car.

Everett had long since purchased a car for himself and his family. He and his family visited his mother often and he worked every day right along beside of James on the farm. Everett had children too and these visits with that family were usually due to work, but were often. Dale Henderson was getting ready to move away and had purchased himself a car a few months back. So now the Dahl car was for James's usage alone. None of the girls or his mother could drive a motor vehicle. The next youngest sister Edith had shown some interest in driving and James was teaching her some of the driving techniques along the way. James simply loved driving trips.

The roads were pretty much curvy between the Dahl home and the sister's house. James loved the speed and the wind blowing through a moving car. Unless, of course, it was dry weather and some other car was traveling just in front of him. That car would be blowing dust straight into the car. It would be so bad sometimes to where one could hardly see the road. James hated that part of the driving trips. Not just because it was hard to breathe, but also because he hated getting his car so dirty. The Model T was black in color and James kept it shining. He felt it was as pretty as it had been the very day his father had purchased it.

Another sister Mabel had been married for a while now and he supposed it would be just a matter of time before she too would have children. James was getting to like this uncle stuff. He was, it seemed at this time, all of the children's favorite uncle. He would get down on the floor and play with them. He would even get down in the mud and play with them. They looked at him as just a bigger kid, only with longer legs.

Although James could be a big kid, his looks were that of a strong man. Being a very handsome young man, he had a body of steel. His dark black wavy hair was long and he kept it neatly combed. His soft loving eyes were royal blue. His face and jaw looked as if it had been chiseled from stone. Yes, Mr. James George Dahl was something to behold. He lived in the sun most of the time and this gave him that healthy bronze shade.

James was quite particular about his clothing as well. By working on his family's farm and helping others with their farms, he had made a little money along the way. There were times James could afford a few nice things that he liked. His choice in clothing was of the finest of dress pants. He liked stiff starched shirts, usually white. The amazing thing about this was that he did not seem to mind ironing those shirts. His mother or sisters would often offer to iron them for him, but James had no problem doing these sorts of things for himself. The way of ironing in those days was by placing an iron upon the stove until it was heated. The iron was of a metallic element that had been shaped into an iron shape. While the iron was heating, one would sprinkle the garments down. A sprinkler was usually a bottle and a cap that someone had made holes in. One would then wad the piece of clothing into a tiny ball. The iron had to be heated to just the right temperature or it could burn your clothes. Acquiring that temperature was a difficult task. Some irons of the period had wooden handles. The Dahl's iron did not. They had to use a towel or a pot holder around the handle during usage. Often one could get burned this way. The Dahl mother wore big wrap around type aprons. She would usually just wad up a section of her apron and use that as a protection. Funny how those aprons could be used for just about everything.

There are several poems about a mother or grandma's apron. These poems tell of how wonderful these aprons were. No one knows all of the words to these poems because there are many. However, everyone knew the uses Mrs. Dahl used hers for. The smaller children would hide behind these large aprons when someone came to the door that they did not know. The big pockets became the same as a carpenter's apron when needed. Sometimes they held small chickens, strawberries or cherries. The large front of the apron could be gathered up to become a basket for bringing in vegetables or anything else that needed toted. The main reason for wearing such aprons was to keep one's dress clean while working. Mrs. Dahl wore a crisp clean apron each day. As she was starting her day, she would stick a nice clean handkerchief under one of the wide straps that covered her shoulder. The apron of many uses also became a heat protector while ironing.

Mrs. Dahl's picky son had to have everything ironed to perfection! James always wore a nice belt and black wing tipped shoes. These shoes usually had white spats covering them. He often wore double breasted suits. He wore stiff, starched white shirts and a tie. He wore a dress hat that he tilted just a hint. In the winter he would wear an overcoat. Due to his broad shoulders, a coat often looked as if it was hanging neatly upon a hanger. This gave a picture of a very handsome stylish man. This young man was an eye catcher for women both young and old. The Dahl family had the reputation of having many handsome sons. There was hardly a lady in the county that would not have preferred one of these young men over all the other suitors available at the time. James may have been at a disadvantage in the neighboring county where his sister Elizabeth lived. The Dahl's were not quite so well known there.

James would often go to church with his sister in the town of Danville. This town was only a couple of miles from his sister's home. James, not knowing many people there would often just lean up against that shinning Model T while his sister visited with the members of the church. This made for a very nice picture. He was a very handsome young man and he did a lot of leaning against that car.

Knowing James may have been a little shy; Elizabeth liked to joke with him. She told him that leaning up against that car so much could make him look lazy. In reality, she was only trying to urge him to get acquainted with the other young people at her church. Elizabeth had, however, remarked to her mother that looking at her big handsome brother standing up against that black shinning car was probably a bit intimidating to the other young men. She always added that he and the car made a perfect picture. Both ladies believed this picture was one that was fit for any magazine.

James seemed unaware of his attractions. He did notice many of the young women watching him. He took this all in stride. He did of course enjoy it. Naturally, he had no complaints about the attention. No complaints at all!

James having many sisters who adored him constantly told him how handsome he was. He was well aware he was a nice looking man. He had many so called girlfriends. Even if he had not been on a date with most of them, there were many young ladies to be chosen from. He did not seem to have any problems finding adorers. He just wasn't in any hurry to find that special girl. This was partly because he had a funny idea. If he did not believe after meeting someone that she could be the one he wanted to spend the rest of his life with, then he would not even ask her out. Often not even for the first time or at least not have a second date with her. Needless to say; this cut his dating time down to almost nothing much of time. Of course, James was still very young and this was nothing for anyone to worry about.

James worked hard on the farm. He and his brothers Everett and Dale planted many crops on the bottom part of the farm. They owned many cattle, some of which were milk cows. They owned lots of pigs, a few sheep and a goat or two. They had many chickens. Mother cleaned and sold eggs. Along with the other animals on the farm they had two large work horses named Clyde and Clude. These were very large, palomino in color, Belgium horses that stood taller than a man. The harnesses alone were too large for most men to handle. James though, with the strength of Samson, could manage them just fine.

The Dahl's raised several gardens and took care of their father's orchard. They did everything possible to provide food for the family. They put up wheat, rye, hay and any other kind of feed or grain they could plant. At this time, they had about four wheat, corn, oat or rye storage bins. Bins were long narrow rooms, of sorts. They could be filled to the top with grain. Sometimes there were little doors attached inside the larger doors where one could open them and dip up buckets full of grain. Others were walk-in bins where one would have large trough like sections full of grain.

Between two bins was a roofed opening that looked much like a garage. It was actually a barn section. There was the first bin, and then a big opening, another bin, then there was an actual garage that housed the Model T. All of this was under one roof. The family kept their newly acquired tractor and other farm equipment in the middle section of this shed.

The Model T garage was starting to look rather funny because their father had started a tradition that all family members had continued. Each year when a tag came off of a car it was nailed to the wall over the cracks between the boards. Ohio had a front and a back tag, causing there to be two tags per year. Everett and Dale were now taking the tags from their cars and doing the very same thing with them. Their father did have a good idea. This habit helped keep the winds out of the garage. During these years no one wasted anything. All materials were put into good use.

Each spring the family would move all equipment out of the shed to shear their sheep in the big open area. This was done by catching the sheep. Someone would hold a sheep's head. Someone else would clip off all of the wool with shears until nothing was left but bare skin. As much as one tried to prevent any injuries there were times one of the sheep would get a small cut. The procedure was then to put a tar like wax upon the sheep to prevent any infections that may have been caused by the cuts. This wax had a very strong odor.

James was so strong to where he could sometimes hold the sheep and shear it at the very same time. Years ago their mother would weave the wool into sweaters, rugs and materials. She had since abandoned that practice when wools became readily available at the local stores. The wool now brought some much needed money into the farm funds. The family would bundle the wool up into a bale that looked much like a bale of hay. They would then deliver the bales to a factory in the neighboring city. The Dahl farm was very self sufficient. It fed the animals and the family. However, it was rarely profitable when it came to having actual money. The large herd of sheep the Dahl's owned really helped to finance the farm's needs.

The brother Everett spent all of his off time with his family. The brother Dale was often visiting with his wife to be. This left James to befriend a neighbor boy. The neighboring family had arrived from the Eastern hills of Kentucky. They had moved to Southern Ohio after one of the Dahl's kin had lost about eighty-eight acres of land to this boy's father. The Dahl relative had lost this land in a card game whilst visiting the Kentucky area for one reason or another. Needless to say no one in the Dahl family was very happy with this relative. They were, however, all happy that the family who arrived there to live on the eighty-eight acres of land was most nice.

The mountain mother was a little lady who wore tall rubber boots under her dress everyday. To say it in the way this little woman would have said,

"I can crawl under fences faster than a youngin'!"

And this was done while carrying a long rifle. This lady hunted all of the time. She did this to feed her family. She was also a good midwife. She had now delivered, as she would say,

"A many of a baby, in this farm country." She told of how she also delivered her own children. Mrs. Dahl could not imagine one doing such a thing.

The lady's husband was a much, much older man. He was way older than she. He had been a widower. He had children older than his now wife. He must have traded or played cards for everything he had, including his wife. It was rumored that this little lady was traded to this man when she was only thirteen. The trade was with the intention that she would become this old man's wife. Mountain folk had different ways. The Dahl's were nice enough to not mention anything about how they believed these practices to be strange.

This family had several children and one son was about the age of James. His name was Clay. James and this young man hunted often together. Clay was quite trained in the hunting department. The boys did a lot of their hunting at night. They called this coon hunting. The furs of the raccoons brought in a good bit of money. That is if you were lucky enough to shoot one. James either did not have the heart to kill such a pretty animal, or he just had not been lucky enough to shoot one to date. He believes it was his heart talking to him. Due to his beliefs, he felt God probably was not pleased with someone killing something they were not going to eat. He believed the Good Lord had placed certain animals upon the earth to feed His people, but to kill for other reasons was not of His liking. James, of course, understood the neighboring family's need to kill for the money. He knew this family was very, very poor. Obviously, they were without farming skills.

Clay's family was mountain people. This family had nothing but an old milk cow and a few chickens. James knew that this, along with the hunting for their food, was their only means of survival. Even if they learned how to farm, their farm would have to be cleared. There were only about three acres cleared for that old house. The rest of the property was nothing but woods.

James went along on the hunts more for the fun of it than anything else. He loved squirrel and rabbit meat and would often bring home some of these to clean and eat. It was common place to see a dressed squirrel in a bowl of salt water around the Dahl household. The meat was tender and very good. During the days when the children were younger they would play with the squirrel tales and sometimes attach them to a hat, just like Daniel Boone.

One night on a fun hunting trip, Clay and James came across something they could not understand, nor explain. They were way back into the thick part of the woods. James remembered when he was a small child that the woods were not so dark or so thick. Instead of forks in the road out in front of his house, there was at one time an old buggy road that went straight on through. There had been some of his family's homes back that way and he knew there was a cemetery somewhere within those woods. He had been told that the cemetery was just full of his ancestors. One of his grandfathers had been a Colonel in the Revolutionary War and received much land for his services to his country. This grandfather was buried in Ewington, but many off-springs were buried in those woods.

James believed his great, great something grandfather had received about five thousand acres of land. By the 1940's many families in this community were descendants of this Colonel. Much of the Colonel's land had been divided amongst each generation. James was not sure of whom may own the woods.

On a fall night, Clay had stopped by to ask James if he would like to go coon hunting. James, grabbing his father's rifle, took out the back door with excitement. He hollered back at his mother to ask her not to wait up for him. He knew she would probably do just that very thing anyway, as she was very much a worrier.

Throwing on his coat, James joined his friend. They crossed the road and jumped over the wide patch of orange day lilies and went straight under the fence. They leaped off into the thickness of the woods for their great adventure. With every step they could hear the leaves crumpling under their feet. James loved the fall weather. It was just cool enough to breathe in crisp fresh air. The leaves were beautiful at the beginning of the fall. After the leaves fell, they made the most wonderful blanket beneath your feet. Ever so often the young men could hear an old hoot owl. Not much light was coming through the thicket, even though the moon seemed very bright when they left the house. Both young men owned some hunting dogs. Well, James liked to call old Trap a hunting dog but he mostly was just a friendly old mute. Clay, on the other hand, had what one would call coon dogs.

For about an hour the young men tramped through the ticket of the woods, sinking every so often into an old stump hole; at which time they would remark of how good it was that they had on tall boots. Clay laughed and said,

"You know James we have never found the end of these woods. What if we could not find our way out? What if we're lost?"

James knew Clay was only trying to scare him and he was not one bit worried. He did not worry because he knew the land pretty well. These woods did seem to go on forever. There were probably more than one-hundred miles of woods. This part of the woods probably went clear to Jackson, Ohio. Jackson was about thirty-five miles away. Although these were facts, there were roads in many areas. Keystone Pike was just over that next hill. James knew all of this because some of his family members still lived there. All of this part of the woods was still part of the Colonel's original land. It was a shame so much of the cleared land had gone back to nature. He also knew if you found the creek, you could follow it home. So James was not too worried about finding his way out of the woods. Maybe Clay really was afraid, James wasn't quite sure. Maybe out of sheer orneriness, James never mentioned to

Clay that he knew the woods very well. He just let Clay wonder.

Both young men were carrying lights and shinning them out in front of them when all of a sudden the dogs went crazy. Clay shouted,

"Now we've got them! The dogs have just cornered some raccoons!"

Just as quickly as he got those words out of his mouth, the dogs did a complete turn around and started yipping while running just as hard as they could back to their masters. Something had scared the dogs almost to death. Both young men stood very still while the dogs were pressed tightly up against their legs. They heard a heavy sound. There were two very distinctive heavy foot sounds breaking every stick and crumbling the leaves in its path. Yes, we said two feet! This heavy animal was walking upright. The young men shined their lights in what they hoped was it's face, but it just kept coming. The lights revealed nothing. What could this be? If only the woods were less dark, one could possibly see the animal.

After a few minutes, or maybe seconds, of being frozen to one spot while listening to the danger coming ever closer, James and Clay decided to run in the direction towards home. They became very frightened. They signaled for the dogs to come. They did not get one argument out of any of the dogs. As a matter of a fact they were moving way out ahead. They would not be of much protection to their masters at this time. They were too frightened themselves.

After much moving and traveling as fast as one's feet could carry them, James and Clay tried to be vigilant as they stopped to listen. Once again they could hear that sound of two large feet stepping very heavily upon the ground. Sticks were popping with every heavy step. True, it was further away from them now, but it was still too close for comfort. The boys caught their breath and moved on ever so fast. Finally, they could see the lights from the Dahl home. As they went under the fence they could see the dogs cuddled up against each other upon the front porch. What could have scared these normally brave hunting dogs so terribly much?

The fellows sat down on the porch step. They tried to breathe better and gather their thoughts. What could that be? Should they have been so scared? They tried to analyze the situation before going their separate ways. After much discussion, they decided Clay should spend the night with James. They decided they had probably made this thing mad. Clay would have to walk down the dirt road to his house. This was about three-fourths of a mile down a hill, around a curve and up another hill. There was much doubt the animal would stop its moving towards them just because there was a dirt road in its path. It would most probably not come near the house because of the lights. Then on second thought, they noted they had lights with them while in the woods. Carrying lights did not seem to scare this animal very much, so house lights may not detour the animal either.

Both boys were wondering just what could be in those woods? Whatever kind of animal this was, it had no fear of people. That was for sure! The animal was not afraid of the dogs and it was not afraid of the lights they had shined into what they believed to be the face. Even though they could not see it they knew it was very, very large.

In their minds eye they knew from the sounds of the animal's feet that it was extremely large. They judged the animal to be over six feet tall and probably weighing several hundred pounds. No such animal existed in this part of the country. They knew this from text books and according to all records and folklore. Different people had told of an ape like creature in other parts of the country. One that made loud screaming sounds. These young men had always felt those were just stories someone had told over a campfire. Neither had put much stock into those rumors. The animal they encountered did not make a sound. It just kept------ on walking. Walking directly towards them!

For nearly two hours James and Clay just sat on that front porch step while gathering their thoughts. They were keeping a watchful eye towards the woods. By now James's mother realized they were home and she had blown out all of the lights. The only light now was the moonlight. Once the lights were off in the house they could see better into the woods. The moonlight was very bright. The young men continued their conversation and their fear. No known animal should have been so fearless. Nothing should have scared the hunting dogs as this thing did. What were they dealing with?

The two discussed this matter until the wee hours of the morning. After much deliberation, the young men decided not to tell anyone. Since they were both still teenagers, they believed people would think they were making the story up just for the fun of it. They also knew they would be teased forever over this one.

So the following day, Mrs. Dahl did not suspect a thing. Clay had often stayed at their home really late. He had also stayed over another time or so when it was storming. But this night, neither boy had slept very well. Actually they had slept almost none at all this night. They kept talking to each other about the monster they had encountered in the woods. Both young men were sleepy most of the next day due to their night of fright. Neither spoke a word of their experience to anyone.

Hunting trips after this encounter were saved for daytime hunts or for early evenings. There were no more midnight jolts into the woods. After awhile, and without telling anyone, life got back to pretty much normal for these young men.

Chapter 3

Elizabeth regularly attended the church close to her home. On James's visits, he always went to church with his sister and her family. On each visit everyone stood around and talked before the services, just as was done at the Ewington Church. On one particular Sunday morning, Elizabeth was busy introducing her brother to any of the church people he had not met as of yet. Since their brother Everett had married a girl from this area, he of course knew the Nash family. Everett's wedding had been held in this very church. Having such a good sense of humor, James was teasing his sister as they were walking into the small church. James's royal blue eyes were dancing while he was trying to focus in on the change of the lighting. He had a hard time focusing while going from the bright sun to the lighting inside of the church.

The morning sun sent rays of sunshine through the stained glass windows of the church. This made it look as if God was showing his presence for the service that was about to begin. As the tall young man let his eyes take in the whole view of the church, his eyes met a pair of the most piecing, very pretty green eyes. The eyes belonged to a pretty petite platinum blonde. Her long hair glistened in the rays of sunshine that was coming through the stained glass windows. James about lost his breath when he looked at her. He thought she looked as one would expect an angel to look. Her pretty little face was so perfect. It looked just like a porcelain doll's face. James could not help but notice she was also put together just perfect. Everything seemed to come together at that tiny little waist of hers. She had on the highest heels he had ever seen on a woman. She was dressed in the latest of fashion. He could not help but stare at her. The young lady seemed to be doing the very same thing with him. She looked him directly in the eyes. He was the first one to look away. This was not on purpose! He had only looked away because Elizabeth nudged him in the side with her elbow.

The whole family was aware of the sensitive section of their brother's ribs. James would often jump sky high if punched even slightly in his ribs. When Elizabeth purposely nudged him there, he groaned and almost jumped off the floor. This caused him to loose his concentration on the pretty young blonde. He looked at his sister and said,

"Why did you do that?"
She whispered to him while saying,

"Ss-h-h-h! Watch yourself, brother of mine. That is the new minister's (<u>ONLY</u>) daughter. She is also a lot younger than she looks."
Elizabeth continued in a whisper,

"I think she is about to turn seventeen, but as of right now she is only sixteen."

James raised an eyebrow at his sister, since he was only eighteen. He could not quite understand the comment about her being so young. He reminded his sister that he was young himself.

34

She had to laugh when that thought struck her. She reached up and patted her brother on the cheek. So often people forgot just how old this young man was. He had to grow up so fast. With a look of regret, she regained her composer and told him that his age did not matter anyway. She believed this young lady was not allowed to date. She believed that she was not even allowed to look at a young man yet. She then said jokingly,

"Oh, if we could have only been so lucky with you in regards to the opposite sex!"

James became quiet as the service began. The minister preached what seemed to be a sermon from way off in a distance. James was coherent enough to know that the minister was much posed and was quite good in his profession. The Reverend had a more city air about him. He spoke more properly and evenly than most country preachers. James knew if he should be quizzed, he could not remember one word the preacher had said that morning. This was because his eyes and thoughts stayed on the back of that pretty blonde's head throughout the entire service. The pretty young lady had now become embarrassed herself. She now refused to ever again look in his direction.

Upon leaving the church, James made a special effort to shake hands with the new minister. He introduced himself. He told the Reverend that he had preached a wonderful sermon, while feeling guilty for not really listening. He flashed a pearly white smile towards the short little dark headed lady standing beside of the minister. It was obvious this was the pretty blonde's mother. She too was a very handsome woman. He noted that she looked very kind. She radiated sweetness. When this lady smiled, her whole face lit up. James made a mental note of her kindness. He felt maybe somewhere in the future she would be a gate to an introduction to her daughter.

Outside of the church, James spoke to the young people he had become acquainted with while on previous visits. There were a couple of his sister-in-law's brothers there. They were always very friendly and great fun to be around. After a little chat, James got brave enough to ask the group what the name was of the new minister's daughter. One young fellow, whom James did not know, spoke up and said,

"Her name is Lucille, we call her Lucy, but I did not tell you that."

He then stepped forward, stuck his hand out and shook James's hand. He said,

"Hello, my name is J.R., or John Herms, Junior. However you would like to say it."

Thoughts rushed through James's head,

"Opps! I asked the wrong person!"

But James introduced himself. The young man continued talking as if not to put a period between his sentences. He said,

"The blonde girl is my sister, and before you get any ideas, she is not allowed to date. My parents believe she is too young. Knowing my father as I do, she may never be allowed to date!" He said this with a chuckle. James did not look deterred! Just about that time a very pretty dark headed girl walked up and took J.R. by the hand. She was telling him of how she wanted him to meet someone who was over by the church. James thought,

"Where did she come from? Wow! There sure are some pretty girls attending this church, maybe I should come more often."

James said goodbye to his friends and walked towards his own family. The nephew Simon was getting big now, but James picked him up just as if he were carrying a sack of potatoes. He placed him under one arm and threw him into his car. He talked over the crowd by screaming at Elizabeth to tell her that Simon was riding with him. The nephew loved this, as he idealized his Uncle James. He bounced into the seat, while giggling the whole time. Just as James walked around to the driver's side of the car; Lucy walked by. She kept her eyes looking downward. James caught the one glimpse she gave him, and took advantage of it by tipping his hat at her. She gave him a faint smile and then looked straight ahead as she kept walking. Her father, sad to say, did not miss one glance or action taken by James. James noticed that the Reverend Herms was staring at him, so he nodded and tipped his hat again as he said,

"Reverend!"

He did this just as the Reverend Herms walked by his car. James could feel the ice in those steel blue eyes that were now staring strongly at him. The man's eyes were of a light sky blue. James had never seen such a color of eyes. Yes, 'Steel Blue' would be a good definition of that color. As a chill went down James's spine, he realized that J.R. was most surely right. This man may never let anyone close to his daughter.

Sunday afternoons with Elizabeth and her family were always great fun. James's sister had made homemade rolls, fried chicken, and all kinds of good stuff from the garden. There was a cake sitting in the middle of the table that was just dripping with chocolate icing. Also sitting close to the cake was one of James's very favorites, a black berry pie, and it was still warm. He joked, while saying,

"Maybe I will just start with my desert first."

He looked over at Elizabeth, who was now giving him what he called the evil eye and said,

"What?"

As usual at a Sunday afternoon meal, James stuffed himself until he felt he could hardly move. Sunday afternoons for God fearing people were times that no one worked. They would only do what had to be done for the survival of themselves and of their animals. They believed in the passage of the Bible that said,

"Remember the Sabbath Day and keep it Holy."

James watched as his brother-in-law went into his bedroom to take his Sunday afternoon nap. Elizabeth came in from the back kitchen and said,

"James, let us take Simon and Ruth for a walk. It is fairly warm today."

His niece, Ruth, was quite a little lady anymore but still tired on walks, so they pulled out the large wicker baby stroller. James helped Elizabeth get the large stroller down the steps of the porch. Once they were all on the ground, they were off for an afternoon stroll.

The countryside was so pretty in the rolling hills of Ohio. Everything was starting to get green early this year. The smells were wonderful and the sun shined brightly. For a while, no one said much of anything while they walked along a path around the small lake that was on this farm. James's thoughts stayed on the morning service. He walked up closer to his sister and put his arm around her as he said,

"I love you Sis!"

She said,

"Okay, what do you want?"

He flashed that big smile down at her and said,

"Would you maybe put in a good word for me with your new minister? **I think I'm in love with his daughter**!"

Elizabeth laughed out loud. Still chuckling while saying,

"I think that happened rather quickly, wouldn't you say? I think I'd better not say any such thing to Reverend Herms at this very moment! Now, do you?"

Elizabeth joked about sending her brother straight home before he could get into anymore trouble. She stated that even though she believed the Reverend Herms to be a wonderful man and a God fearing, wholesome person; she would bet when it came to his beautiful daughter there was probably a tiger inside that neat three piece suit. She reminded him that the Herms family had only one daughter and three sons. Yes, she knew that the daughter was very beautiful, but she also knew he should watch his step around this situation. She noted that the Reverend Herms was already keeping his eye upon him. She had noticed the watchful eye the minister was giving her handsome brother.

Elizabeth informed her brother that other than being the most handsome young man she knew, she wanted him to know he was not by himself in waiting for the hand of Miss Lucy. She told him,

"You know you are not by yourself, every young man around here has his eyes on that one." She went on to tell him of how the difference being, each of those young fellows seemed to have enough sense to know when to back off. Each of them knew that it is a 'no go' at this time. She warned him that Lucy's daddy would put a stop to any kind of flirting before he could say,

"Hello, my name is-----!"

James stretched taller while throwing his head high. Once again he flashed that smile at his sister and said,

"Oh Sis, ye of little faith! I've already introduced myself to her father and her older brother. It is just a matter of time now!"
Elizabeth just shook her head. She believed it had become a challenge now to her little brother. So, trying to talk him out of his pursuits would be hopeless. She did tell him that she hoped he would honor her parent's wishes and not approach the young lady until she was at least seventeen. He laughed at his sister and said,

"Why, what do you think I am? Do you think I am a cradle robber?"
She looked up at her baby brother and laughed as she said,

"You are hopeless! You do know that don't you? You are just hopeless!"

Elizabeth's thoughts wondered as she thought of how the family may have put too much pressure upon this young man? Everyone, including James, believed himself to be older than the young age he really was? She realized he may be older than his years. Yet inside, she knew he was still just a child. She felt a mixture of sadness and pride for this character she called her brother. It saddened her that he had to grow up so fast. She did however have to laugh at his brave ideas. As Elizabeth laughed out loud, James laughed too until he finally realized he did not know what they were laughing about, so he asked,

"What's so funny?"

Elizabeth just shook her head in laughter and said,

"YOU!"

She shook her head (no) until a frown came over his face. She then said,

"Never mind little brother, I just want you to know I really, really love you. I love you because and in spite of your courage!"

Chapter 4

For the next several months, the farm took all of the Dahl family's time. Spring and summer were full of raising gardens and planting fields. Elizabeth and her husband were busy on their farm as well. Visits were far apart during these busy months.

The world seemed to be going crazy. There were wars going on in different parts of the world. Paris had been captured now by Germany. The United States was still staying neutral, but did take measures to assist China and the Western Allies. The American Neutrality Act had been amended in November of 1939. This was to allow cash and carry purchases by the allies. During this year the United States had increased its Navy significantly. The United States embargoed iron after the Japanese incursion into Indochina. Most Americans opposed any direct military intervention into the conflicts. People knew after the tripartite pact between Japan, Italy and Germany, if you had a problem with one, you would have to fight all three.

Foreseeing the possibility of a coming conflict, many young men in the farm areas were signing up for the Navy. Some said they preferred the Navy over the front lines. They figured if the strong farm boys did not enlist quickly then they would, more than likely, be the ones in those front lines if they waited to be drafted. James believed everyone was panicking before anything happened. He believed from reading the news, all of the people of the United States was in agreement to stay out of the war.

Life went on as usual at the Dahl farm. Fall was finally here and everything had to be harvested. James's sisters Edith and Bella were both of high school age now and were of a big help around the farm. Most of the time, everything went smoothly for the Dahl family. James would notice fellows at church flirting with his sisters a lot of times, but he usually knew how to handle that. He was so much taller or larger than most of the local boys to where one word from him would usually cause them to back off. One brave old bachelor, from across the way, would upset Edith a lot. He was way too old to be thinking about younger girls. He must have been shy and missed his time in life to date a young girl. James had run the man off after he had brought some flowers and candy to Edith. He was a good fifteen years older than her. This man had walked across the back field to give these things to Edith while the family was harvesting wheat. The thought that he would have walked across several farms to reach this field was unnerving to James and the girls. Not wanting to worry their mother, they made a pact not to tell her. Their mother was such a worrier. It was decided that James, Dale and Everett would have to keep a watchful eye on this character.

Their sister Mabel had married into a neighboring farm family. She lived in a house way back off the road, but it was just across a fence to the back of the Dahl property. She had worn a path across the field from her trips to her mothers. Mabel and her husband split their working time between the two families and helped with all of the harvest work. The two families then would supply the young couple with all of their home needs. James felt sorry for the young couple, especially when he found Mabel had made rugs out of feed sacks to keep the floors warm. He had told his mother about this. She then in turn had told her friend, Mrs. Wyman who was Mabel's mother-in-law. She or his mother, he wasn't sure which one had now provided a nice large wool rug for Byron and Mabel's living room.

The brother Everett and his wife Hazel had two children, a boy just a little younger than Simon and a daughter just a little younger than Ruth. Sadly, they had lost two other children at child birth. This was hard and very sad for the entire family. They did have funerals and the boys were buried in a corner lot just above their father, their brother John and their sister Gwen. Now, Hazel was expecting another child. This caused her to not be of much help on the farm. Mrs. Dahl being the worrier that she was, insisted she would watch Hazel and the children while Everett worked. This really meant that she would try to put Hazel to bed all of the time. Hazel was, of course, a little reluctant to do this but she would come along with Everett and bring the children. The children would often ride along in the wagons behind their dad and uncles while they worked.

The Dahl family was so very close. They would work hard, pray often and enjoy each other's company. They always tried to remember to laugh as hard as they worked. James usually kept them in stitches. Even with all of the grief this family had endured, all of the children ended up with a wonderful sense of humor.

Mrs. Dahl did not work in the fields much anymore, but it was as if she was always taking on more work. She took her duty of seeing that Everett and Hazel were to have a healthy baby to extremes. One had to feel sorry for poor Hazel. She was to do nothing for nine months but stay in bed, according to the forceful, watchful eye of her mother-in-law.

Mrs. Dahl took care of the house, the chickens, the laundry, the cooking and the gardens. She also took care of her grandchildren. The milking was still a big chore of hers. Edith would tease her mother by calling her a milkmaid. This woman got up at five o'clock every morning and worked until nightfall. All of the children worried about her. Now the butchering and canning season was upon them. She would not be able to rest until November. Even though they worried about their mother, this big wonderful family would never miss a beat at teasing her. They loved to tease her about her speech every morning as her feet hit the porch. Their very serious mother would shout,

"Everybody up, you are burning sunshine!" She had been doing this now for thirty years, by now it had become a habit. It must have worked too, because no one ever dared to sleep past 6:00a.m. The now adult children were very well trained.

Chapter 5

This year Elizabeth had come to a couple reunions through the summer. She had come to visit a few weekends along the way. But the Dahl family, including James, had not been able to go to Elizabeth's home to visit with her and her family. It was mid October before James got to take the old Model T and travel to Danville where Elizabeth and her family lived. His mother and his younger sisters tagged along with him on this trip. They too, wanted to see the family. Their brother Dale, once again, was off to see his fiancée. Elizabeth had been complaining about not being able to meet her new sister-in-law to be. But, the fiancée lived too far away for Dale to bring her home with him very often.

On this day the family arrived early enough to where they were able to go to the church that Sunday morning. James was disappointed when he found that the Herms family was out of town to visit relatives. The church had a guest speaker on that morning. However, he did get to visit with Hazel's brothers. He learned a lot more about the Herms family. The pretty little blonde had now turned seventeen. The church had thrown a big birthday party for her.

The Nash boys were laughing at James for his interest in every little detail of Lucille Herms's life. One of them said,

"Wow, you've got it bad! Don't you?"

As the teasing continued, they told him they believed someone had beaten him out of the running. They ask him if he remembered the pretty dark headed girl. They were describing the girl who had grabbed J.R. away from their conversation during his last trip to the church. Well, it turned out that J.R.'s girlfriend had several brothers and sisters. This one sister and one brother were pretty close to Lucy's age. The one brother was very sweet on Lucille. The Nash boys realized this disturbed James. It disturbed him a lot! Even so, they knew they must continue to tell him about the situation, so one continued by saying,

"The brother had sat with Lucille on a couple occasions at church."

They told of how they had also seen him talking to her outside of the church at different times and after several services.

Unbeknownst to James there had been a young lady watching him all morning. At this time she was walking up to their group. She was none other than the other sister of the boy they were speaking of. She was very pretty in her own right. This young lady knew the Nash boys. She spoke, while smiling at them. She asked,

"Who's your friend?"

They introduced James to her. Her name was Opal. She stood around and talked for awhile to all of the boys. It was very obvious she was interested in James. James did seem to be somewhat of a flirt! He carried on a lively conversation with the pretty young lady. The Nash boys laughed as one whispered to the other,

"I don't think we need to worry about him!"

After church, James and his family went back to Elizabeth's home where they had Sunday dinner and played with the children. These were always wonderful times, but James seemed to be down in the mouth today. His mother ask what was the matter. Before he could answer, Elizabeth answered for him. She laughed and said,

"Oh mother, James has a major problem today. Has he not told you of the beautiful blonde he claims to be **in love** with over here?"
Mrs. Dahl answered,

"<u>No</u>! But there does seem to be some sort of a distraction over here. I am having a hard time keeping him at home."

Elizabeth was having a heyday at her brother's expense. She said,

"Well mother he claims he fell in love with this pretty little girl the very first day he met her. The only problem being, he has not told her nor has he asked her father for permission to see her."
James, who was sitting at the table with the others, leaned his chair back onto two feet and locked his hands behind his head. He knew if he did not say something his sister was going to chop him up and eat him for dinner. He flashed those pretty white teeth as his eyes started to dance with mischief. He then said,

"Mother, Sis is only half right, I have introduced myself to her father. Step one is completed."
Elizabeth said,

"When are you planning on telling mother that her father is my minister? Were you planning on leaving that little fact out? You also need to tell her that the father did not seem to be too terribly fond of you in that so called introduction!" He just laughed and said,

"How could he help but love sweet little ole' me?"

Their mother just shook her head and got up from the table while carrying some dirty dishes. Elizabeth did the same thing and gave James a sort of side smile. Then she gave him a look that he understood to mean that she believed he was just hopeless. She confirmed that thought by saying,

"Baby brother, you are beyond all belief. Your courage may just override your better judgment one of these days."

Their mother hollered back from the kitchen and said,

"Boy! That is for sure!"

They all had a good laugh.

James jumped up and sat the heavy chair back down on all fours. He ran to his sister Elizabeth. He towered over her by at least a foot. He gave her a big squeeze just as he lifted her up from the floor and said,

"Just who are you calling baby brother?" His mother said loudly,

"Put your sister down before you hurt her." Everyone, including mother, was having a wonderful time this day. Elizabeth's husband usually just stood and watched these family interactions. He always kept a big smile on his face, but today, you could hear a chuckle now and again. Things must have been getting extra crazy today, because most usually Mathew would excuse himself and go for his afternoon nap. Today the brother-in-law seemed to be having as much fun as everyone else.

After much fun, the visit had to come to an end and everyone had to say goodbye. The little kids were jumping up and down. They did not want their Grandmother, their aunts and Uncle James to go home. James, his mother and sisters had to start back home before it got too late because they wanted to complete their chores before dark. That probably was not going to happen today as they had stayed way longer than they expected. The days were a little shorter during this time of the year anyway.

Elizabeth stood at the door and asked them to please bring the others, Dale, his fiancée, Everett's family, Byron and Mabel on their next trip. James laughed and said he could not fit that bunch into his car. He stated that they would just have to come sometime on their own. No one seemed to complain at his suggestion. Possibly they were just too tried to fight the situation. Not much was said on the way home either. Both James, his mother and sisters were just basking in the fun flavor of the day.

The next couple of months glided by, then Christmas came and went at the Dahl household. It had become common practice for all of the children to be home for Christmas Eve. The family had a long standing tradition of gathering a tree for the glorious occasion. This was usually done on a day or two before Christmas, so everyone tried to be at home in time to do this. They hooked up the big horses, Clyde and Clude to an old buckboard wagon and the whole family would go out into the woods to find a tree. They would sing Christmas carols along the way. They took along hot chocolate and cookies. This was great fun for all. The little kids, while all bundled up in their coats, scarves and boots, enjoyed this trip so very much. The trip became all the better if they were lucky enough to have snow on these days. On the snowy days the family would take the large sled instead of the wagon.

Many stories were told about Santa Claus along the way. Mother was getting so she wanted to come along on this trip. When her children were growing up, she never seemed to have the time. Now, there were no little ones left. James and the girls were the babies of her family. The preparations she used to stay home to do, she now had plenty of help. Everyone else seemed to be involved in those preparations at this date. She had more than enough help with the popping of the corn, the stringing of the berries and the making of ginger bread men. So, it was good she could go along on their family excursion. Besides, the Mother Dahl would always make sure the true Christmas story was told to the young. The whole story time was not taken up by just Santa Claus and his reindeers.

On these joyous days of the holidays, the family took the time to remember the part of their family who were no longer with them. They would join in a circle of prayer and hope the others could somehow know they were thinking of them. They had a practice of putting a shoe under the tree. This was because they had nothing but a pot bellied stove which made them unable to hang stockings on anything such as a mantle. The family had continued this unique practice all through their years. One extra shoe was placed under the tree for each of the two siblings who had passed on. For many days no one would touch the candies and the oranges placed within the brown paper bag that was slide down inside of those shoes. Finally someone would separate the goodies amongst everyone. This was just another wonderful way to remember their loved ones.

Mabel always seemed to be the reader for the family. She would gather all of the little nieces and nephews around her chair and read to them. The same two books were chosen to read from each Christmas. Those were: 'The Night before Christmas' and 'The Christmas Story from the Bible'. Each child would sit there in anticipation with big bright eyes shinning as they waited for their aunt to start reading. These wonderful children slide closer in as they listened to each and every word. Not one child would look away as they were feared they may miss a word of the stories.

The family usually spent several days together. They were always pretty exhausted after the holidays. This year no one seemed to mention having any kind of celebration for James's birthday. His birthday was on the 27th of December. It was as if all had been forgotten. James did not mind! His mother always remembered his birthday. This year she had surprised him by baking him his own cake. This year he did not have the normal left over Christmas cakes. When his birthday arrived, the whole family did sing to him. Each and every one of them told him,

"Happy Birthday."

His sisters, Bella and Edith had both made him cards. So his birthday was pretty nice even without a big celebration. The family wasn't too concerned with a New Year's celebration either. The Wyman's had a nice party and Mabel had invited everyone to her in-law's home. The Dahl's did attend and everyone had great fun.

James learned his friend, Clay, had joined the army. He had stopped by in late February to tell everyone goodbye. The service was sending him off to another state for training. Dale had received his service papers in the mail recently as well. The government had stamped these papers with a rejection notice for the time being. The papers went on to explain that Dale Henderson was a son at a farm home. There was also a statement on the front page of those papers that stated,

"Son of a widowed mother."

Dale had full intentions of joining the reserves, so he was relieved with that piece of news. James figured it would all be the same for him when the time came to get his notice. He had heard the army was not going to take any young men like him.

The papers did arrive just a few months after Dale's. These papers had read,

"A Farm Boy, Baby Son of a Widowed Mother."

James would not be drafted. The government had left a clause in the paperwork that allowed for further consideration if need be. They left an option for his future listing if needed. As of right now the papers received were of a great relief to Mrs. Dahl. Everyone had been living in fear that things were going to get worse in the wars throughout the world. Mrs. Dahl knew that Dale planned on joining the National Guards, but somehow felt he would be safer in that branch of the service. This branch usually stayed close to the home front.

Early spring came and the family started getting out and about. They were going to have an addition to this big loving family before long. Everett and Hazel's new baby was coming soon. Everyone was so excited about this. Everett, Dale and James had talked of how they wished it to be a boy. Everett having a boy as the oldest, a girl as the second child, a boy should just come next in line. This was the thinking according to these young men. A little odd for rationality, but no one ever accused these boys of being rational.

SHE; finally arrived! It ended up being another girl. The strange thing was that none of the three young men seemed to remember they had wanted a boy instead. The baby girl was so very beautiful. She reminded everyone so much of their beloved Gwen. Gwen was their sister who had died the day before her twenty-first birthday. Their sister Gwen was so dainty. She had jet black hair. This beautiful baby girl was also dainty and she had the blackest of hair. The family felt that God had sent her to them as a reminder of their beautiful Gwen. Mother Dahl said,

"Gwen has chosen her for us from all of Heaven's babies."

The mountain mother who lived on the next farm had delivered Everett and Hazel's baby. Mrs. Dahl had made a remark to her of how she missed James's friend Clay. Clay's mother had tears building up behind her eyes. She dropped her head so no one would notice as she said,

"I miss him too. I miss him so much!"
She then told of how she prayed everyday for her son's safety. She said she prayed America would

not join the wars. Then as this mountain family always did, she started humming a tune. She hummed 'Amazing Grace' as she busied herself with Hazel and the baby. Music was such a part of Clay's family life to where it must be their comforting medicine. Mrs. Dahl knew talking about Clay made her friend sad and she was now afraid this conversation would make her miss him even more. Mrs. Dahl felt so sorry for this family with their son off somewhere without knowing when he may return. She felt a relief that none of her sons were in that situation. James's mother made a mental note of how she had always liked that young man Clay.

This mountain family was very talented. During warmer weather they would sit on their front porch of evenings. They would play instruments and sing beautiful country songs. They sang so pretty. The music just seemed to radiate out over the countryside. While neighboring families were doing their chores, the music would flow through the valleys. This would serenade the Dahl family while they worked. Mrs. Dahl had always liked hearing that bass voice of Clay coming in so strongly. The girls and another brother still sang beautifully by themselves as they played their guitars, fiddles and banjos each night. The songs were pretty and the voices were lovely. The young people could make those instruments talk. The whole family sang in harmony. The old man played the Banjo. This family should have been known in city circles. The Dahl's were very sure that Clay's family could have become very rich with their music. Since there were no radios and no electricity in the area, these evening songfests became a wonderful form of

56

entertainment. Their singing was something the neighboring farmers looked forward too.

The cities and villages had radios and people there could keep up with all of the news and listen to new music. There were a couple of comedy shows out now. There was also a drama or two that came across the airways at this time. The Dahl's wished they could soon have electric run out to their home. It had reached as far as Vinton by now. That was only three miles away. The children having lots of friends there, those they had gone to school with, now had electricity. The Dahl children visited with their friends every chance they got. On these visits they got to enjoy the modern day radios. They would always come home with great excitement. They would tell their mother all about the shows while repeating many of the skits they had heard on the radio.

Electricity might as well have been a thousand miles away. The fact was that the electric companies would keep going. They would complete the lines up the highways first. Placing poles and stringing wire up dirt roads for a mile or two probably would not happen for another few years. In all reality, it just was not feasible yet. Farm people lived anywhere from two to five miles apart. Granted, this was true on the roads called highways too. The difference being however; the electric companies had to go up the highways to get to the towns that were strung about five miles apart. In Gallia County the roads they were calling highways were only different in the fact that they had lots of mashed in river gravel. They may have also been a good bit wider in size. Most of the farm roads were just dirt and almost impassable at certain times of the year.

Knowing that the usage of a radio was way out into the future, the Dahl's made due with the victrola and a few old records. Of course the Dahl family liked to sing and play instruments as well. Their instruments were of a much different kind than the ones used by their neighbors from the mountains. The Dahl's considered themselves to be playing and singing just for fun. They felt the mountain family sounded more like professional entertainers. The Dahl's owned a piano, a coronet, a trumpet and some violins. They were quite good on all of these instruments with the exception of the piano. Edith and her mother were the only two who tried to play that. The children had been well trained on the other instruments while in school. The Dahl's had never heard anyone play guitars and banjos before. They also got a big kick out of the mountain people calling violins, fiddles.

It was sort of hard for the Dahl's to understand these mountain people because they were not farmers. The family wanted their farm to stay wooded. All they had was a garden. A large garden, of course. One that fed their family. They had a few chickens that they used for eggs. If an old hen would hatch some chickens and the family felt they would not jeopardize the flow of eggs, they would eat a chicken once in awhile. They had no other farm animals other than one old black and white cow. They used it for milk, butter and cheese. Most of their protein was hunted out of the woods. It was guessed that the family probably bought chicken feed of some sorts and maybe some hay in the winter for the cow. They really did not know.

The Dahl family raised everything they needed to keep up their large amount of animals.

They had very large fields of rye, wheat, oats and hay. Clay had explained that where they came from it was very mountainous and thickly wooded. He told them it was hard to find a spot to put a garden, much less plant anything else. For generations the families from all over those hills had lived as his family lives. He told that his family had been lucky because they were fairly close to a little one room school house. He and his siblings were fortunate enough to be able to attend school. He told of how most of the mountain folk lived too far back into the mountains to attend schools. Though their ways were somewhat odd to the Ohio families, this was just the mountain folk's way of life. It had been their way of life for decades.

Chapter 6

Spring passed fast this year. 1940 had just disappeared. Now the days of 1941 were moving along just as quickly. James had all but forgotten the summer when he spent so much time with his sister Elizabeth. Planting season was about over now and he was starting to get off the farm on occasion. He had been a few places with the Woods girl from down the road. She had sat with him in church and seemed to believe she was his girlfriend. His sisters had told him as much. She had given him a picture of herself and had written on it, Love Sarah. He felt, in his own right, that one could hardly call the rides to church a date and wondered why she would think they were dating. He had carried his mother and two sisters along every time. He guessed maybe she had counted the couple trips just he and she had taken to Vinton to get a soda, or something, as sort of a date. He was going to have to watch that sort of thing. She was, however, someone of his own age and was lots of fun to talk to. He just hoped she was not getting serious about him. He wanted her for just a friend. Besides, he would never want to upset her wonderful grandparents whom she stayed with during the summer months. The grandparents were wonderful family friends and great neighbors.

One beautiful Sunday morning, James, Dale, Everett and all the rest of the family went to Elizabeth's for a full days visit. Mother had fixed lots of food. She stated of how she could not expect Elizabeth to cook for such a large group. Everett, Hazel and their children were going to church with the Dahl family. They were then going to split their afternoon between Elizabeth's and Hazel's family.

As everyone arrived at the church the large Dahl family along with the Nash family took up about three rows of seats. They all had been very happy to see each other. The families had joined together while visiting out front. The services were about to start when this large group moved to inside the church. Naturally, everyone in the church turned around to see who was occupying so many rows of seats.

James saw what he so wanted to see almost immediately. That pretty blonde was there with her brother's girlfriend and her sister. The girls sat alone. All three turned and smiled at James as he sat down. A quick turn and they were facing forward again as the service began. The service went on smoothly while all of the time James, once again, could not take his eyes off the back of Lucille's head. She had on a pretty lavender color dress. It had lace on it. She had a bow in her hair made of the same material with lace upon it. James got lost in the minute while thinking of how very pretty Miss Lucille Herms was. He knew, in reality, all of those girls were very, very pretty. Why could he not get that particular one off his mind?

After church, the two large families walked down the steps together. The nephews, John and Simon, were about the same age. The little boys got between Everett and their uncles. They were jumping up and down. So, the men took the boys by their little hands, lifting them both off the steps so their little feet could not touch the ground. This took up the whole wideness of the steps and was quite a site to see. The three very handsome young men, who were all dressed to the nines, carried the two pretty little boys down the steps. Everyone in the parking lot was watching them. Lucille was in the crowd and laughing along with everyone else at the young men's show. James smiled directly at her and Lucy gave him a big smile back.

Elizabeth walked up and said,

"Simon, if you and your cousin do not throw one of your loud spells, I will make some homemade ice-cream this afternoon. James, being the child he was inside, whispered something to the boys. Then, both James and his two nephews let out a big, loud,

"Yeah-Ha!"

Elizabeth smiled and just shook her head. Their mother jokingly apologized to everyone who was standing outside of the church. She said,

"I would like to apologize for my loud family."

The whole crowd acted as though they were being entertained. They all laughed and acted as if they were enjoying it all. Then, each family member got into one of the cars and left the church parking lot.

That afternoon passed by very fast. James and the family had enjoyed every minute of the visit. It was starting to become evening and they would have to leave soon. The chores at home would not complete themselves. So, the family hugged and kissed everyone goodbye. They thanked everyone for a wonderful day. James told Simon and Ruth that he would bring them each a toy on his next trip. James and Dale helped their mother and the girls put all of the pots and pans that they had brought full of food, back into the car. The family loaded up. As they drove off they were waving and blowing their horns.

James had this little problem. His mother often called his little problem a lead foot. He wore a size twelve, but one should not blame his heavy foot on the size of his shoe. The young man just liked speed. As he approached a curve on this winding dirt road, he did not slow down much at all. Apparently another car, had another lead foot driver, and was coming from the other side of the curve just as fast. As they approached each other in the opposite direction, it looked as if they would surly crush. Everyone held their breath! Both cars had to come to a complete stop and then back up to let each other pass. To give each driver the benefit of a doubt, these country roads were just perfect for one car but when two cars met it was a very tight squeeze. If one moved over too the far left or too far to the right while letting another car pass, they just might end up in a ditch.

As each driver approached the other for the second time and both had moved over just enough to squeeze by, they both stopped to apologize to each other. As their windows lined up, James said,

"I am sorry for that and I hope I did not scare you!"

A nice looking young man hung his head out the window and said,

"Look buddy, I'm guilty too, I just love driving these roads."

James recognized the young man and said,

"Hey, didn't I see you at church this morning?"

At about that time James noticed the passenger in the other car. It was none other than Miss Lucy! That beautiful blonde was smiling at him. His heart sunk! Thoughts came crushing down around him. He realized this must be the young man everyone said they had seen her with. Obviously, she was allowed to go on dates now!

While in that disappointing frame of mind, the other young man cut into his thoughts by saying,

"Well yes, as a matter of fact you did. I don't think we have met. I'm a son of the new minister.

"WOW!"

Brain flash James,

"What did he just say?"

James could feel relief wash over him. It felt as if a title wave moved from the top of his head to bottom of his feet. The weight of lead had been removed. This young man was none other than another of Lucille's brothers. Someone had said there were three brothers. His mind was doing flip flops. Elizabeth had told him that there were three sons and one daughter. It just took a few seconds to soak in.

The young man was saying something else while James was snapping back into reality. James was a little embarrassed that he had become so rattled. He was sure it was showing all over his face.   The other guy stuck his hand out of the window to shake hands with James as he said,

"Hi, my name is Lewis."

Turning to Lucille, he said,

"This is my sister Lucille.   I'm the third child of Reverend Herms.   I have an older brother. His name is John.   We call him J.R.   Then there is Lucille here and a baby brother named Henry."

He then asked,

"Aren't you Mrs. Stewart's brother?"

James gathered his composer and said,

"Why yes I am, my name is James, James Dahl."

He then reached out to shake hands with the nice young man.

To keep the conversation going James let the young Mr. Herms know that he had already met J.R.   He then told the two in the other car that he was very pleased to meet the both of them. They just sit in the middle of that curve talking for awhile.   James introduced his mother and siblings. He told Lewis there were nine children in their family.   He then said,

"Two have passed on and out of the seven left you will find I am the nicest."

James always joked when he was nervous.   He noticed Lucy laughing at him.   She then spoke and said,

"Well Mr. Nicest Dahl, it is very nice to meet you as well!"

Everyone in both cars laughed.   As Lucy was joking with him, James could not help but notice that she had, beyond any shadow of a doubt, the prettiest smile he had ever seen.

James realized very quickly that just being around Lucille Herms could not be putting him in the best of light. He could not even remember what he was saying from one second to the next when he was around her. The brother was talking again and James was lost in that smile. After hesitation, he did decide on what he believed Lewis was saying. He was asking if James would like to come to visit some Sunday afternoon while he was at his sisters. He said that he and the neighborhood boys often got together on Sunday afternoons. He said,

"We can play horseshoes or something." Embarrassed again for his lack of concentration, James quickly said,

"Yes, I'd like that very much. It is a pleasure that you asked me."
Then he leaned over to look at Lucille and to keep her attention, he said,

"Once again it has been a pleasure to meet you and I hope to see both of you again soon." Lucy said something about Lewis not being old enough to drive and it was getting dark. So, they all waved goodbye. Each sped off in opposite directions.

Chapter 7

All week long, James could not get Lucille Herms off his mind. He tried by picturing different girls in his mind's eye to see if he even knew anyone as pretty as her. 'Nope'! Couldn't think of one, actually he could not even imagine anyone that pretty. He'd ask himself questions like,

"How old is she now anyway?"

He did wonder about that for a minute. He started counting in his mind. Being detail oriented, he wanted to know within months. He figured her to be about seventeen and one-half right now. Didn't someone say her birthday was in April? She sure looked like a woman. Everything on her was put there perfectly. He guessed her top and bottom had to be about the same size. Then she tapered down into the smallest waist he had ever seen on anyone. It seemed every dress he had seen her in to this date was made with a really wide belt. That seemed to show her waist size more. Her legs looked long and perfect. Yet he knew without the high heels she probably wasn't taller than 5'3" or 5'4". There must have been a good four inches on those shoes.

It is a wonder James completed any of his duties during that following week. His mind stayed on that girl named Lucy. His mother had asked him upon several different occasions this week if he was coming down with something. He would just answer,

"No."

But he knew he had come down with a very big case of the longing, needing, wanting and could not live without that girl. His mother and others kept asking why he was so quiet this week. He stayed in his own little world while thinking about Lucille Herms. Questions were asked of him all week. With his large sense of humor he would answer his family with something stupid like,

"I'm just trying to get done with my work before winter."

This would leave a bewildered look upon everyone's face. They would walk off like they thought he had completely lost the last little bit of brain he might have.

The following weekend went by the very same way as the past week had with James thinking of nothing but Lucille Herms. The family went to their home church in Ewington. The Woods girl tried to talk to James. He did come to his senses long enough to realize that maybe he had hurt her feelings. He suddenly realized he had hardly given her two words. She stood around waiting for him to ask if she wanted to ride home with his family. But, when he didn't say anything, she hopped into a car with another family that lived close by.

James knew it would be a few weeks before they could be visiting his sister Elizabeth again. He also knew the farm, his mother and siblings were his responsibility. Not that any of them were helpless. Far from that, he just knew he had to take responsibility for his own actions and concentrate on his daily duties. Doubts started crossing his mind. He thought he saw caring in Lucy's eyes, but he had been told of that other boy. That young man lived so much closer to her and he was a friend of her family. Someone told him the girls often spent nights at each others homes. How could he compete with that? Was Lucy already committed to that other guy? He knew if he didn't quit letting these crazy thoughts roam around in his head, they would surely drive him mad. So he tried to think of other things. BUT, no matter how hard he tried every thought came back to Lucille Herms.

Monday started off as every week with his mother at the wheel of life. What a remarkable lady she was. This tiny little woman still worked circles around everyone else. Each morning from the minute those shoes, with the noisy taps upon them, hit that small concrete patio she went non-stop until bedtime. His mother just never quit, she was the last one to wear out at night. By the time she had awaken everyone else in the house, she had already milked the old jersey cow and had prepared a big breakfast and spread it out upon the large family table. The morning was no further along than about 6:00 a.m. by that time. What an amazing woman his mother was.

This Monday morning, James was slowly moving. This was because he had not been sleeping very well lately. Every since that last encounter with the woman of his dreams, he had not been able to go to sleep. Instead, he would play little scenarios in his mind of Lucille Herms being his wife. He would even see them in their own home with children all around them. He knew at this point if he lost his chances with this young lady he may never want another woman. He felt it was his destiny to be with this girl and with this girl alone.

About three weeks had passed. The last week had been unusually busy. This had taken James's mind off his love life for a little while. Fall was setting in and James's family had to get the crops in. They had butchered a hog. Then they had made apple butter. Both of these events were big deals. Each took a lot of effort and concentration. James's mother, his sisters, and his sister-in-law would boil water. When the hog was ready, they would dip it into the boiling water. Usually the largest pig had been chosen to butcher and this was a very back breaking work process. One had to dip up and down into the water. James would usually do this task. Dale or Everett always helped, as it would take more than one person to hold the pig. After the dipping, everyone would get into the act and scrape off the hair from the animal. Many things were done with different parts of the pig. Big hams were cut, then salted and hung inside of the smokehouse. The skin would be used by cutting it into stripes. Then the skins would be fried in large pans full of lard. Lard was the fat that was taken from the pig. Much of the lard was also saved in big buckets to be used throughout the year. This was the only shortening the family used. The skins would fry up wonderfully. These skins would make a very nice snack treat.

Some of the pork had to be canned. Most of it was smoked, salted or sugared. Once all cutting was done, it was placed into the smokehouse to hang from the ceiling. It was then to be smoked or whatever means of preserving they chose. It was considered stored right where it hung. Once the actual butchering was over, it seemed most of these jobs were left to the women. Finally, it looked as if the hog work was done. This year James had done most of the cutting up of the meat. He had been very careful with the skins so his mother could make the pork rinds. He always looked forward to this treat each year.

Another task was the apple-butter. Apple-butter was made by putting the apples and all of the ingredients into a very large copper kettle. Kettles were most usually of a five to ten gallon size. The Dahl's owned a ten gallon size. This took an awful lot of apples, plus the ingredients. The kettle hung over an open fire. The Dahl's had a stand made at an ironsmith's shop. This stand held the kettle in place. The contraption stood in between the circle part of the driveway that went out to the barn. It was quite a process to get ready for the making of the apple-butter. Not to mention the work it was while cooking it. They had a big lathe wood paddle. The handle was as long as a broom handle and looked very much like one. The bottom part was a very thick board with circle holes cut into it. The holes were about the size of a penny. It put James in the mind of a school master's paddle. The ladle probably had about ten holes. The reason for all of this was for easy stirring. Someone would stand and stir. Stirring went on about all day. While the apple-butter slowly cooked, the family took turns stirring. Some of the women could hardly move the heavy tool. After it was completely done, the women would put the apple-butter into the canning jugs for storage. A red wax like material would be placed on top of each jug for sealing purposes.

These past few weeks passed by quickly. The harder everyone worked, the faster it seemed to go. There was still much to be done before winter. The family still had to butcher a beef. That in itself was a bigger job than the pig. There were also many things yet to come out of the orchard. All of the produce had to be picked and canned. The family also had hickory nuts and walnuts to pick up. These items also had to be stored. Thank God, most of the grains had already been harvested and were stored safely away.

Everyone had been so very busy. The evenings were filled with fun and lots of joy while visiting with each other. All their loved ones were staying at the house until all the winterizing and work was done. This was common practice for this large family who had grown up on this farm. Everyone carried their load. Everyone worked very hard. During these busy times, James did not have much time to think about Lucille Herms. This was not because of his choice, it was just because he would fall fast asleep the minute he put his head upon a pillow.

During the fourth week James went down the road to his uncles to borrow his sauerkraut cutter. When he left their farm, Dale and Everett were cutting heads of cabbage in half. The cabbage had been planted late this season for some reason. When James returned he found that his brothers had cut up enough cabbage to feed an army. He noticed that mother had the salt water ready. He knew this because when he walked up, Edith and Bella were having a very fun time putting eggs into the large jars to see if they would float. He then realized the salt was most probably placed into the big pottery tubs by his sisters instead of his mother. Mother would have never tried more than one egg. Then he remembered the rule of floating an egg on salt water. That practice was more for the summer pickles, not necessarily for sauerkraut. He laughed as he wondered just what the kraut would be like this year. Hopefully not so salty to where no one could eat it. One relief was that he had the pleasure of dipping out a lot of the brim. He replaced it with plain water before starting. Besides once the cabbage became kraut, it would have a lot of juices of its own. Thankfully this would thin out much of the salt. Thank goodness, the girls had only placed about one gallon of their invented mixture per each five gallon jar. Even that was entirely too much. James had to remove the biggest part of the brim before even starting the slaw process. As he was dipping and dumping the brim over the side of the jar, his sisters stood watching him with their hands over their mouths. He heard one of them say,

"Opps!"
He could not help but laugh at his precious sisters. They were having so much fun.

James realized the Dahl family was a very big family! Some of this food was to go to Everett and his family. Some was to go home with Mabel and her husband, but he could not understand why that much kraut. They had to use three five gallon pottery jars this year.

Everett, using the cutter, cut the cabbage for awhile. Then Dale cut for awhile. Then it became James's turn. He cut for what seemed like hours. Funny thing, he noticed there was no one to relieve him from his duties at the time he felt he had done his share. He sat at those jars a big part of the afternoon. Bella stood by while waiting for him to finish. Her job was to take a big bladed chopper, that was actually a long knife, and chop up and down inside of the jars. This was to make sure everything was cut finely. She sang to him while she waited. They always had great fun while working together. They heard someone coming and looked up to see Edith with the big crockery plates that were to be used to weigh the brim down. Finally this job was completed. Once again this family was exhausted. James cleaned up the slaw cutter and handed it to Everett so he could take it back to their Uncle Andy's as he went home.

Before going into the house for dinner this evening, James noticed the traveling store was coming up the hill. The owner of this truck-store also owned the feed store and a general store in the next town. One never knew when he would arrive, but he tried to get past everyone's house at least once a week. The store keeper usually brought along with him, his pretty daughter. James knew she was attracted to him. She liked the looks of Dale too. Both had often flirted with her shamelessly. Dale got so he would not go near the traveling store anymore since he was planning on getting married. This is one evening James knew he would be too embarrassed to go out to that truck. He was dirty, he was tired, and he really just wanted to hide somewhere.

The Dahl family had bought a twenty-five pound bag of salt from the gentleman last week. Now they knew they would not need nearly that much. They had more salt and vegetables than they had jars. The vegetables, like pickles, could be canned if mother so desired. They did not need that many summer pickles. James knew there were more jars out by the barn, but he would have to walk way out there and carry, or roll them to the yard. He also remembered they had sheared sheep close to those jars, meaning it would take awhile to get them sterilized enough to use. Then after thinking about the one to five years of dirt collection; James thought it would just be easier to return the unused portion of salt. So, contrary to his wishes, he went out to meet the truck. To his surprise, Mr. West's daughter had not come along on this trip. James was so relieved.

James just wanted to quit this evening. It had been a very hard day. He started to get enough water out of the rain barrel to clean up his being, but remembered he had already been chewed out for that once today. It saved so many steps in comparison to walking around the house and pumping water. His mother had caught him getting water from the rain barrel earlier today and that had not gone over very well with her. His mother had hair of silk that fell down below her waist. Her hair was very long. She usually wore it atop her head in the form of a bun. It was turning grey anymore, but it still shinned like glass. The reason for the shine was because she had never used anything but rain water on her hair. The daughters used the very same rain water for their hair. This rain water came from off the roof of the house and was kept in a big barrel at one end of the house. James did understand why his mother got upset with him earlier in the day. He was just tired and he still had lots of chores to do before turning in. But he gathered his tired body and slowly walked around the house where he grabbed a bucket and pumped himself some water.

All of a sudden it started to rain. Dale, in a sour kind of way, made a remark of how GREAT this was! He grumbled something about how now they would have more apples fall from the trees. The rain was coming down pretty hard by this point, but the chores still had to be done. Bella came running from the chicken house telling of how there was a hole in the roof and her baby chickens were in a tub container. She sounded panicky as she told of how they had gotten soaked from the rain. Everyone else had started out to the big barn by now, so James ran out with Bella to check out the problem. James and his sister dumped the water out of the container. The chickens were so small and so wet to where their little feathers were just drooping. Bella looked like she was going to cry at any minute. The two decided they would have to take the little creatures into the house. After reaching the house, Bella said she was going to stay in and dry them off. James went to the barn to help Dale and Edith.

Later, as the family sat down at the dinner table, James noticed mother had not made any bread or rolls this evening. He started to ask why, but he remembered the wet baby chickens that he and Bella had brought into the house earlier. Bella and their mother had wrapped the chicks in a blanket and had placed them in a cool oven over top of the heated water tank. The water tank was on the side of the coal stove. The hot water kept the oven above slightly warm. This is usually where mother would place her bread to rise. She had started, but did not attempt to finish her bread tonight all because of the welfare of the baby chickens. Livestock was the Dahl's livelihood and they would always come first over someone's desire to have bread with dinner.

The family knew they would have a good meal without their much loved bread. James knew this even if he did, pretty much, believe a meal was not a meal without bread. In a sneaking little thought he remembered where there was one piece of bread left over from a big meal they had had when all of the family came to help last week. If he could get to it first, he just might survive this meal. About that time Mrs. Dahl put out a big, good looking mince meat pie. Now everyone was going to be just fine without any bread and the chickens just might live to grow up. That is, of course, if they were able to stay warm the whole night through. The family said their blessings over their meal and everyone knew no one would ever go hungry at the Dahl household.

Chapter 8

Friday came and went. Saturday was a very busy day. Mrs. Dahl was out at the clothes line with a club beating the daylights out of some rugs. James walked up to her and said,

"Hey mother, what did these poor ole' rugs do to you this time."
She laughed and stopped to hug his neck. She said,

"And I suppose you, son of mine, are done with all of your chores for the day. Am I correct?"
He said,

"No, I just stopped to ask you a question".
She said,

"Okay, go ahead."
He asked, or maybe he suggested she go with him to his sister Elizabeth's on that Sunday. She did not answer him directly. She loved her grandchildren and would love to see her daughter and her family, but she hated to miss going to her own church. She even taught a Sunday school class and this would put a burden on someone else. James kept quiet while he knew his mother was thinking it all out. Finally she told him to go ask Dale and the girls if they wanted to go. He did that right off and then came running back. He told his mother that his siblings did not want to go this

Sunday. They all had other plans. His mother got into deep thought once more. She finally agreed that it would be nice to go for a visit. However, she could only do this if Mrs. Woods was willing to teach her class this Sunday, and at such a short notice. She told him he would have to go ask her.

James loved to go to Mr. and Mrs. Woods. Bella did too, so he asked her to come along. They lived way back off the road. Their house was one of the last log cabins in the area. Everett and Hazel lived in one, but theirs had almost fallen down before they went to work on it. They had remodeled it so much by now to where it looked like an everyday house. The Woods cabin, on the other hand, must have remained just as it was built. The family had taken such good care of it.

James often wondered if the Woods were maybe relatives somewhere back in the distance. He had heard the first two story log cabin that was ever built in this area had been built in the 1700's after the Revolutionary War. It had been built by James's Great, Great something grandfather. It was believed this cabin had been in the neighboring town of Ewington. It was also believed that it had long since been destroyed. This was most probably true. But that fact did not keep James from wondering if maybe the Woods cabin was also one his grandfather had built. Two story cabins in this area were very uncommon. Originally James stubbornly thought maybe people confused where the cabin had been. All of these lands once belonged to the Colonel. Plus there was the fact that Ewington was not a village at that time. The tiny town was only two miles down the road. So-o-o, who knew!

Mr. Woods had told James many times that his wonderment was completely wrong. To top that off, his Uncle Andy had told him he was wrong. The uncle had to tell him several times before James could get those thoughts out of his brain. Finally, he started to believe maybe there was two cabins since his Uncle Andy had told him that he could remember the old cabin that was over in Ewington. The uncle told of how the cabin was still standing when he was but a boy. James had to laugh at himself for being so stubborn about that silly cabin. Surely others knew how to build a two story cabin. That talent could not have been left to only those members of his family.

James was happy to know that the Woods owned a very large and a very nice two story log cabin. James guesses his thoughts on the cabins lingered with him so long because all of the cabins in the area were either being torn down by now, or people were building houses around them. This was done to the point to where one could not tell there was ever a cabin inside of them. Loving the old cabins as James did, this saddened him.

Like all the farms in the area, the Woods did not have electricity. By the time James and Bella arrived, oil lamps were lit everywhere. The clock, just inside their door, bonged seven times as James and Bella were welcomed into the house. James could not help but think of how much quicker it seemed to get dark down in the valley. Maybe it was all of those trees. The two storied log cabin had a fire place that covered a whole wall. It was so big. One could walk into it! There was a glistening fire burning in this fireplace as they approached the living room. The whole house smelled wonderfully of baking bread.

Mrs. Woods came out of the kitchen with a big smile upon her face. She wiped her hands on the corner of her apron. This jolly little old lady looked round. She was round faced, round bodied and as big around as she was tall. The couple had been married so long to where it was like that old saying;

"If you stayed together long enough you would start looking alike."

Mr. Woods was equally round; with the difference of having a pipe hanging out of one side of his mouth.

The Woods were very happy to see the Dahl children. They ask them to visit with them awhile. James had to quietly laugh inside when he remembered what Bella had said to him on the way down to their farm. She had said,

"Mr. and Mrs. Woods remind me of how Mr. and Mrs. Santa Claus must look."

The Woods children had all grown up and left home. They had the one granddaughter who would stay with them from time to time. Most of the time they were just alone. They had visited and saw each Dahl child immediately after their births. The sweet old couple had been there through all of the Dahl family losses. They had been there to hold their hands and grieve right along side them. They were wonderful neighbors and wonderful friends. The Dahl family truly loved Mr. and Mrs. Woods. To Mr. and Mrs. Woods, each Dahl child was as if that child were a family member of theirs. They especially cared for Bella. She was the baby of the family and the jolly old couple babied her every time they saw her.

Mr. Woods said,

"To what do we owe this wonderful pleasure?"

Mrs. Woods reached out for big hugs and ask them to please sit down. James told her of his reason for the visit and she kindly offered to teach the Sunday school class that Sunday morning, getting that out of the way right up front. Mrs. Woods thought it was nice that their mother could go visit with her daughter and grandchildren. She insisted that the children stay for some warm milk and a piece of cake. They were both delighted to do so. Mrs. Woods made the best cakes in the county.

James pulled up a chair to the fireplace along side of Mr. Woods. Mr. Woods was such an interesting person to talk with. The old man remembered so many people and happenings of the past. He told James so many stories. He told about how the countryside looked at the turn of the century. He told of how the buggy road, which is now all grown over, had once came right in front of their door. There had been a four way crossing at the Dahl's home instead of a three way. He explained how once the road got into really bad shape, that was when people quit using it. This caused their place to be back in the woods with nothing but the long driveway.

Mr. Woods said he was not complaining! He told of how sometimes it was really nice the way it is. He seemed to be undecided about this because he continued by saying,

"However; sometimes it can be lonely without visitors."

Unless one was coming directly to see Mr. and Mrs. Woods, one would not know the house was back there. Mr. Woods would tell of how the road used to go clear over to Keystone Pike. He guessed the county just did not want to keep the road up anymore. Maybe it was really hard to grade a road that went up and down a steep hill like that. He told of how there had been two or three other log homes on that very road at one time. He believed after everyone had died off, no one else was interested in living so far back in the woods. Nature had gradually reclaimed her land and gently retired one log cabin at a time.

James knew about this story and found it funny that Mr. Woods always wanted to tell him again. Maybe the old gentleman was trying to remind someone that they should maybe take care of the cemetery he would always tell about. He was an old man now. He told of how he could not go back there to keep it up as he once did. He wished someone would take over those duties and care for those who had all but been forgotten. He reminded James of this every time they spoke. Repeating himself, he would say,

"There is a cemetery back in those woods."
Just as if he were telling James this for the very first time. He would tell of how it once was right along side of the now missing road. He acted very concerned as he told James of how the cemetery had grown over. He was sure it had become a terrible mess. He was so saddened at the thoughts of how hardly anybody even knew it was back there. He would then say,

"Boy! Do you know there are a lot of your ancestors back there?"
He would just shake his head and say,

"Such a shame! Such a shame!"
Then as an after thought he would say something like,

"You know Sarah Dahl is buried back there, don't you?"

I overheard some of your family at church one day saying no one knew where she was buried. James knew the answer to that by now because some of his family members had found she was buried in the Ewington cemetery, but to disturb the old gentleman with that news would be futile. James made a mental note of the old man's information just the same while thinking that maybe there was more than one Sarah Dahl. James nodded at Mr. Woods as if to acknowledge.

In all reality, James knew very little about the Dahl side of his family. All he knew was the things his Uncle Andy or someone like Mr. Woods would tell him. His father had died when he was so very young. Uncles and Aunts would stop by from time to time, but most of them lived far away anymore. They never stayed in close contact with the family. Most of his childhood relations were with his mother's side of the family. They visited all of the time and everyone on that side was very close. James's family had stayed so busy on that farm and mother was so very sad over her loses to where not much was said about their father's side of the family. It was always nice to talk with someone who knew everyone and knew things about those who had now passed on. Therefore, Mr. Woods's stories were always welcomed and quite wonderful to listen to. James could listen to this old man for hours and never get bored.

All of a sudden, James heard the clock bong nine times. He said,

"Lord of mercy! Have we been visiting this long?"

Bella looked perfectly happy over in that corner. She loved visiting with Mrs. Woods. James motioned for her to come and told her it was time to go home. He felt mother would be worried. They said their thanks for the delicious cake and they said their goodbyes. They told Mrs. Woods their mother would be most thankful for her agreeing to teach her class. They then headed for the door. Mr. and Mrs. Woods told them to hurry back. They ask them not to stay away so long the next time. They both told the young people of how very much they had enjoyed their visit.

When the siblings arrived back home, they bounced into the house rather loudly. James screamed,

"Hey mother, Mr. and Mrs. Woods send their love and yes, Mrs. Woods will teach your class."

Mrs. Dahl came into the kitchen and said,

"Why all the noise? Some people in this house are asleep."

James guessed Dale and Edith must have already gone to bed. Mrs. Dahl said that it was nice of Mrs. Woods to teach for her and mumbled something about how if Mrs. Woods was not so old, she would have liked to give her that class. Then she said something about herself having it way too long now. She continued with something about the fact that James always had to run, bounce, and scream out all the time. She said,

"You just wear me out."

He knew his mother must be extra tired this evening, guessing from the things she was saying. So he just kissed her on the forehead and said goodnight as he headed up the stairs for bed. He could hear Bella telling her mother, in a calmer voice, all about their visit. He still wondered if their mother wanted to hear so much about their visit at this late hour. But he felt that would be Bella's problem.

James worried about his mother anymore. She seemed to be tiring out more easily. Just this morning, she had remarked something about all of his energy. He had made a remark after something she had said. He told her of how he usually had a hard time keeping up with her. She had slapped him on the shoulder and said,

"Is that right Mr. Dahl?"

Then she took off in almost a run towards the house to prove a point. He knew his mother loved him very much. This feeling was mutual, as James adored his mother. He felt like her big protector. Often though, he wondered who was protecting who. The older brothers and sisters often remarked of how James was Mother's favorite. He knew this was not true. He also knew that he got a lot of her attention because he was her baby boy. The truth never stopped his siblings from teasing him constantly about this. Mother would always let all of them know that she had no favorites. The charming lady would joke with her children and tell them of how she loved them all very, very much. Then she would say,

"If I had not loved you all so much, I would have dropped each and every one of you, one at a time, off upon someone else's doorsteps."

The family would always laugh at that, while knowing they were deeply loved by their precious mother.

Chapter 9

Sunday morning finally came. James had completed all of his chores much earlier than usual. He figured it was the excitement building up within him. This was caused by the up coming visit to his sisters. This is the first time in his life he was up before his mother's milk run to the barn. Maybe it was because he was cold this morning. The weather had turned very chilly in the evenings at the Dahl farm. The upstairs, where he slept had become very cold over the night. The wind had been blowing pretty hard. Last night it felt as if there were no windows in the upstairs part of the house. The structure was open all the way through from one window to the next. It was only separated by curtains hanging here and there to give privacy. The slanted ceilings were covered with varnished wainscoting boards. The ceiling came down to within about two feet above the floor at the side walls. There seemed to be nothing used to insulate the upstairs of the house. The floors were of a varnished planked wood.

The upstairs looked more of a dormitory than a children's bedroom. Due to the large family, this old upstairs had reared each of the children into adulthood. There were two full size beds on each side of each window. Then there were a couple of beds in the middle of the upstairs. As each child would become an older teenager, he or she would get moved downstairs to the extra bedroom down there. The oldest always got the small bedroom between the sitting room and mother's bedroom. Sometimes two children, close to the same age would have to share that room. Of course, meaning normally it would be two brothers, or two sisters. Most of the time it was occupied by only one child.

The upstairs was always very clean. It was a cabin style room and it was very pretty. It went the full length of the house, with the exception of over the kitchen. Their father had added the new kitchen to the house in his later years. This house was way over one-hundred years old. Mother would often tell a story of how the house had a tree growing up within the parlor on her first visit. Now, due to their parent's hard work and devotion, this house had become a very beautiful home.

Mother Dahl had used much material to create curtains for the children's upstairs bedrooms. The curtains were used for partitions between the beds. These curtains created little rooms of sorts for the one or two children who slept behind them. Mrs. Dahl had sewn heavy weights into the bottom of the curtains to keep them from blowing around so easily. The double layers of canvas helped with the installation of the cold upstairs. When the heavy canvas curtains were pulled back, the rays of sunshine shined through this pretty upstairs. It became magical with all of the colors of the different quilts, flowers, and mobiles that the children had hanging upon the walls.

There was no one left anymore to sleep upstairs except James and his brother Dale. Dale was leaving soon, so James figured it would all be his before long. Both of the younger girls, who were still at home, slept downstairs. The two young men had chosen beds close to the end windows so as to be far apart. This was probably not too smart during the winter months, because the wind came in around those windows. The only heat to the upstairs was from the brick chimney. It came up through the middle of the upstairs over by the stairway. Of course the pot bellied stoves had to be burning to cause that to heat. This was only the fall season and no one had built a fire to date. They had not even moved the one stove back into the parlor yet. Everett had reminded them to oil it down and get it back up before it got too cold. He informed them he had already put his into his home. He would be comfortable regardless, as he had a large log cabin fireplace. James wondered why he had been in such a hurry to get his stove up since there would be no worries about heat for Everett and his family.

In this upstairs, there were wood airplanes hanging back under the lower parts of the ceiling. There were also a few wooden trucks, trains and a stuffed doll or so. Most of the wooden toys, in those areas, had been made by their father or their older brother. Since both were deceased, the items would be saved forever. The family would keep these items right where they were as long as a Dahl family member lived in this house. The toys were dusted often, but they were never moved.

Stuffed away in the magical old attic were many trunks that were packed full of memories. The Dahl mother would never part with any of her memories. Her wedding dress and her husband's wedding suit were tucked neatly inside of one of the trunks. Many old fashioned shoes and coats filled the drawers of these trunks. Behind the old trunks was a large picture. It was framed with a nice glass cover. Inside the frame were butterflies. This creation had been created by their deceased sister Gwen. Directly in front of this picture stood an opened trunk filled with all of her personal belongings. Ever so neatly placed, laid a beautiful crocheted bed jacket. This jacket had a note pinned upon it. Written on this note was a sentence that said,

"Made by your Aunt Ethel!"
Aunt Ethel was their father's sister. Aunt Ethel had passed by now as well. The Dahl children knew each and everyone of these precious belongings were of most importance to their mother.

In the sister Gwen's trunk, the first thing you may see would be a black leather book. This book had been hand created by Gwen. It was tied together with rawhide strings. This was a book of poems that their sister had written. She was quite the poet. Although James, Edith and Bella hardly remembered anything about these poems, it was very nice to hear them read. Mabel would often get the book out of the trunk during her visits. The whole family would gather around her while she would read these poems to them. Gwen would have been very pleased to know her gesture of leaving these poems to her sister Mabel had paid off. Mabel did not have the heart to take the book to her home, even though everyone knew the ownership was hers. She could not bear to take such a treasure away from her mother even though her mother had told her upon several occasions that it would be okay. Mother made it clear to all siblings that Gwen had written, during her illness, that she wished her sister Mabel to have her poems.

Everyone missed their sister Gwen and mother had saved everything that was dear to her. Of course mother had much of their deceased brother's belongings in those old trunks as well. Some of the trunks were saved for the living. They were filled with music sheets or music books that were used by all of the children. There were a couple of old violins and bows nesting inside of their cases. These violins stood statuses along the wall. There was a trumpet and a coronet. Both of these items belonged to James. He still played them often. He had been considered the very best first trumpet player in his school band. It was a shame he had to quit school early. The whole family was rather musical, it seemed. Deeper within those old trunks one could find every school book or Sunday school lesson any of the children had completed. This old upstairs had once been so full of laugher. The large second floor had once been the bedroom to each and every one of the nine Dahl children.

This morning was fairly chilly, but James did not notice it so much once he got up and moved around. He was quite comfortable by the time his chores were done. Upon leaving the barn, his mother turned the corner. She jumped as if she were frightened. He told her he was sorry! She told him that was okay and that she was just shocked to see him out there so early. She then laughed and said,

"You must be very excited about our visiting trip."

She, obviously, was in a mischievous mood this morning as she ended that by saying,

"Or-r-r, could it be that little preacher's daughter?"

He just grinned and said,

"A little of both mother."

Then he headed for the house. On the way to the house, he thought of how if mother only knew that today he was going to try to win the heart of that little preacher's daughter. He was going to take her brother up on his offer to visit. Before this day was through, he hoped to be a fixed item within the Herms household.

Everything smelled so-o-o wonderful as James stepped into the house. Mother had everything warming upon the stove. The food was waiting to be finished and served. James rushed upstairs to clean up. He decided he would find the very nicest thing he owned to wear this morning. He knew, with this weather, he had better not dress too warm. Even though the evenings were starting to get cold, the days were still quite warm.

As this young man was getting dressed, thoughts came into his head that he had pondered upon before. How was he going to approach the Reverend Herms? James had been raised only by his mother and the older siblings every since the young age of ten. What was it like to have a man running the house? What was it like for a strong man, like the Reverend Herms, to be the head of a household? He also kept remembering that Lucy was the man's only daughter. This was going to be very tough! Yes, very tough indeed!

The more James thought about things, the more worried he became. But, he also knew he had no intention of giving up on his wishes. He truly believed that somewhere out into the future, he was going to make Lucille Herms his wife. Talk about determination. This young man was determined. He tried to keep up his confidence this morning; mainly because he was scared at this point. The time was drawing near. He was scared for so many reasons. Not just for the reason of having to talk to Reverend Herms at some point in the near future; but also scared that the young lady may already care for someone else.

Other than the obvious concerns, the Sunday morning was going along pretty smoothly. There was a worry for James about a certain white shirt. Once his mother came back into the house she told him to quit panicking. She told him that his favorite shirt was clean. It was pressed and in a downstairs closet. She tried to keep quiet as she suppressed a chuckle. She had just realized where that picky dressing came from. Her thoughts wondered back to the day when she first met her beautiful husband. She remembered that he had looked like he had been pressed, folded and all starched up himself. She could never forget the neatness of that handsome man. Obviously this trait must be an inherited dignity.

Finally! All clothes were on everyone's backs and all were looking spick and span. James and his mother were well on their way to the church in the next county. James was very quiet, but was driving very fast. His mother asked him to please slow down. She, in the year of 1900, being just seventeen at the turn of the century, did not feel she was equipped to fly down dirt roads at such high speeds. Cars had always given her great fear. James slowed down just as his mother asked, but he remained very quiet. His mother reached over and felt of his forehead. She asked,

"Are you coming down with something?"
He just smiled and said,

"I'm fine, Mother."
Mrs. Dahl was not one to leave anything like that alone. So she asked again,

"Are you sure you're not sick."
He snapped at his mother this time by saying,

"I'm in perfect bloody shape mother!" Almost immediately he realized that was very rude and he apologized to his mother. She said something to the fact, about him not being too old to take out behind the buggy shed. She then said,

"The word, <u>bloody</u>, is something I wish the Dahl family had left in England, Scotland or wherever they're from!"
James felt badly that he had upset his mother, but his attitude had left the door open to where she kept chewing on him now. She told him that <u>bloody</u> was the one word his father had used that she did not like. James kept apologizing and told his mother that his nerves were just on edge this morning. He knew he was being difficult and vowed to correct that. He had put so much stock in his plans for this day. He was so very tense. One might say that he was wound up tight as a rubber band.

Approaching Elizabeth's house, James and his mother could see from a distance that the family had already left for church. Mother told James if he had not lollygagged around while getting dressed this morning, they would have been there on time. She was giving him what he

98

called 'The Look'. He sped up again so as to arrive at the church on time. This time his mother did not object. Yet, when they arrived at the church most everyone had gone inside. The last bell was ringing. James took his mother's slender little hand into his and said,

"I love you mother!"
They then walked into the sanctuary.

As James and his mother located Elizabeth and her family, they were able to slide in behind them. Simon climbed over the seat to be with his Uncle James. Before James could get seated, Simon tried to jump into his lap. The tall young man bent over with one scoop and picked his nephew up onto his broad shoulders. He was not thinking of how the young boy's shoes may be dusty. He did not think of what that would do to his shirt or his dark pants.

When James realized what had happened, he put Simon down onto the floor immediately. He started brushing the dust and dirt from his sleeves and his pants. Just as he looked up again, he saw Lucy Herms coming down the aisle. As she passed, she gave him that beautiful smile. Her green eyes were twinkling. She surprised him as she laughed and made a comment to him,

"I think you got most of that!"
James, not being prepared for any of this, just stammered something about how nice it was to see her again.

As everyone sat down, James collected his thoughts. His mind was racing as he thought,

"Okay, that was embarrassing."
What was she going to think of him? It seems every time she sees him, he is doing something silly or something out of the ordinary. Was she

going to believe he was forever acting too much like a child? Or would she believe he was too vain? Oh well, it was too late now, she had already seen him in a volatile state. He could only hope that she was going to overlook all his flaws. He certainly hoped so. Maybe she had already overlooked his flaws, because it seemed every time he looked at her, she would look back and smile. James was hoping that was a good sign.

All through the service, James's thoughts stayed on Lucille. He noticed the girls who sang for the service were very good singers. They were sisters. One of them was J.R.'s girlfriend. Although James's mind was always way off with Lucy somewhere, he realized the good Reverend Herms was quite a good preacher. James tried harder to focus on the sermon this morning. Simon sat beside of James throughout the entire service. James's mother looked at her son with a worried look. She once again asked James if he was feeling well. Elizabeth heard her mother's concern and quietly chucked. Their mother got a surprised look upon her face. Then they both turned their knowing eyes towards Lucy. The mother shook her head up and down as to acknowledge that she understood what Elizabeth was trying to tell her. She smiled with relief while knowing her son may really be sick, but it was love sickness.

Church ended with everyone shaking hands and saying their goodbyes. Mrs. Dahl was speaking with Mrs. Herms. As James walked up, his mother said,

"This is my son, James."

Mrs. Herms answered by saying,

"Yes, I believe I have met your son."

She then turned to his mother and said,

"What a handsome young man your young James is."

"Thank you."

His mother said, with a proud smile. She was always appreciative when someone gave one of her children a compliment. James reached out to shake the Reverend Herms's hand at about that same time. He felt an extra strong grip as the older man pinched his hand. Lucy's father griped much tighter than a usual hand shake. It was almost as if the gentleman was angry. This embarrassed James somewhat, so he anxiously walked out the door.

James was hoping to see J.R. and Lewis this morning. Several young men were leaning up against some of the cars in the parking lot. As he came down the steps the boys spotted him and headed in his direction. As he reached out to shake hands with J.R., Lewis walked up as well. Both young men told James that it was good to see him again. J.R. laughed about the encounter James and Lewis previously had on the roadway. He had been told about the experience. He started remarking of how Lewis was far too young to drive and of how no one should have allowed him to do so. He then told James of how thankful he was that no one hit the other. Everyone had a good laugh.

James did not wait for either of the brothers to say anything about today. His being very nervous caused him to immediately blurt out what he wanted to say. He said,

"Lewis, I thought I would take you up on your invitation today! That is if you do not have any other plans."

Lewis said,

"Sure, we would love to have you, we have no special plans."

J.R. tuned in by saying,

"I fear it will have to be after 2:00p.m. A church family has invited our family to lunch today."

James said,

"Great, that will be fine. I will see you then!"

Just as James tipped his hat and walked towards his car, J.R. said,

"Hey! Do you even know where we live?" Everyone laughed. James had to laugh too because he had no clue of where they lived. Everyone was still laughing when J.R. put his arm straight out in front of him. He shut one eye as if he were to site, then he used his finger as if it were a gun. He pointed as he pulled his index finger back while making a clicking sound with his tongue. He was pointing at a big white house across the street. There stood a very pretty two storied white house. It had a big wrap around corner porch. James said,

"Very Nice!"

J.R. made a large bow and said,

"Compliments of this lovely church. Before you stands my humble home."

James said,

"2:00p.m. it is then!"

As everyone went their separate ways, James was thinking of how much he liked Lucy's brothers.

Lunch at Elizabeth's was wonderful, as usual. It was so nice to see mother having fun and relaxing. This was something she rarely did. James loved his precious family. He was thankful

102

they were all so close. He talked with everyone while he played with the children. He could not help but think 2:00p.m. was never going to come.

Time finally did pass and James made his excuses as he headed for the Herms's home. James arrived at the Herms just minutes before the family pulled into the driveway. Everyone spoke to him as each family member got out of the car. Reverend and Mrs. Herms were polite enough towards him while they headed toward the front door of their home. James thanked the young men for inviting him. Then the boys headed towards the backyard. The Herms boys already had the horseshoe posts set up. It looked as though these posts had been there for quite sometime. James realized they must be pretty good at this game. The grass was missing a good two to three feet out away from each pole. Someone picked up the horseshoes and they started playing right off. J.R. was first. He never missed, not even once! James thought of how he was in trouble and hoped no one would judge him on his poor ringer ability.

The boys played for a good while and James was feeling very inferior about his playing ability. He remarked of how happy he was they were not playing for money as he would have been broke an hour ago. After a while, Mrs. Herms stuck her head out of the door and asked,

"Are you boys having fun?"
They all hollered back and said,
"Yes!"
That little lady, with her big smile, had to be one of the nicest people James had ever met. She was also one of the shortest ladies he had ever seen. Snapping James back into reality, J.R. asked,

"Mother, do you have anything to drink?"
She said,

"Yes! Why yes I do!"
He said,

"I would like to offer something to our guest."
His mother said,

"Of course, I was going to do that very thing."

Within a few minutes, Lucy came through the screen door with a tray that had a pitcher and glasses upon it. As Lucy got closer, James could see that she was carrying homemade lemonade. He was sure that would definitely hit the spot. However, his mind was on the pretty server. As she handed him a glass full of lemonade, his mind started wondering to how he was going to ask her out.

"Should he go to her father first?"
Probably so! He guesses he best find out if she wants to go out with him first. The smiles and the looks he had been receiving from her made him believe she was interested in him. How could he be sure?

Miss Lucy had not really been flirting with James. He knew how other girls acted around him if they were interested. With Lucille Herms you really were not sure. She acted so different. It was so hard to read her. Maybe this was all because she could tell she had him dead to right. Or maybe it was because she knew she was beautiful and did not have to put up any effort for the fellow she may wish to have. He got so many butterflies in his stomach when he was around her. He felt he probably sounded really stupid every time he opened his big mouth.

Everyone took a break while they had the very good, cold lemonade. After they each put their glasses back onto the tray, and to James's surprise, Lucy left the tray right where it was. She picked up a horseshoe and threw it. It was a dead ringer. James screamed,

"WOW!"

J.R. laughed and said,

"Oh that is nothing unusual, she beats me all the time. She is the best of all of us at this game!"

He then asked,

"You want to play Sis?"

She said,

"Sure!"

Then she bounced off while taking the tray back into the house. She ripped off her apron and came running back outside. The game was on! J.R. certainly was correct! This gal could play! She never missed. Every time she hit a dead ringer. One would hear that big CLING... Lucy would laugh and she would go again. She knew she was impressing James. She would throw her head back and laugh out loud. James's legs seemed to shake the whole time. He loved the sound of her laughter. He knew his nerves were shot and he knew it was because he was basking in her beauty. He had dreamed, so many times, of being this close to her.

The afternoon was fun. Really, Really, FUN! Like all good things, it had to come to an end. James knew he was soon going to have to leave the Herms household to pick up his mother. He also knew the Herms would have to go in for dinner soon. They would have to get ready for church. Lucy hung around with them most of the afternoon. She talked. She laughed and acted as though she was one of the boys. It all seemed so natural. He supposed she was so comfortable because she was raised with all boys. There was such closeness between the siblings. Not unlike his own family.

James decided he was not going to leave without finding out where he stood as far as Lucy was concerned. The boys were telling him how much they had enjoyed his visit and of how they hoped he would soon come back for another. James looked over to Lucy and said,

"Well, I'm definitely not a threat to you as far as winning. Now am I?"
She laughed and said,

"No, please do come back soon."
This was music to his ears. She showed she was happy he came.

As soon as James arrived at Elizabeth's, he knew it was time to go. Mother was waiting on him. On the drive home, mother asked him if he had fun. He told her that he did. He stated,

"I had a wonderful, wonderful, wonderful time!"
Then before she had a chance to ask, he got a silly grin on his face and said,

"Yes mother, I have been invited back!"
Mrs. Dahl laughed and bopped him on the back of the head. They both laughed most of the way home. Yes, today was a most wonderful day! A wonderful day indeed!

Chapter 10

Lucille Herms attended a high school in a little town called Rutland, Ohio. She had a friend who lived straight across the road from the school. Most lunch hours, she and her young friend would go across the street to have lunch at this girl's home. Lucy would always pack her own lunch, but it was far more fun eating at her friend's house instead of on the school lawns. Lucy had become a very close friend with this young lady. She would often visit with her on weekends. Her friend Sally would often come and spend a night with Lucy. Then in return, Lucy would go spend a night with her and so on.

On the Sunday afternoon of December, seventh of nineteen and forty-one, Sally had stayed the night before that date with Lucille. She had attended Sunday school and church with the Herms family. Lucy's brother, J.R., was to take the young lady home after the services. Lucy was to go with them. He was going to go on with his girlfriend to her brother's home for lunch. Eve's brother also lived in Rutland. J.R. was then to come back by Sally's home to pick up his sister.

This Sunday was going along as usual. Lucy really liked Sally's family. The girls had a nice lunch together and then they settled down in the parlor to listen to the radio. This was always great fun for Lucy. Her family had a radio, but it was rarely turned on. The Herms family was more of the outdoors type. They rarely listened to a radio.

Just as Sally's father turned the knob to find something interesting, he stopped on NBC. The NBC Red Network was broadcasting 'Sammy Kaye's Sunday Serenade'. The show was with Sammy, his Orchestra, Tommy Ryan, Alan Foster, and the Three Layettes. The girls liked the music, but they knew the broadcast was just about to finish. It was just announced that the following program was going to be a rather bland program called, 'University of Chicago Round Table'.

Sally and Lucy did not even attempt to take a chair. They knew this was not something they cared to listen to. They were pretty sure that Mr. Cartwell would want to listen to this topic. So, they were preparing to leave the room. The topic of this program was going to be '<u>Canada - A neighbor at war</u>'.

Canada, a part of the British Empire, had declared war on Germany very soon after England had done the same. The United States supplied materials to the British. Canada was supplying an even more precious commodity, (Their very own young men). Just as the girls started to leave the room, they heard an announcement that said,

"BULLETIN!"

"BULLETIN!"

"NEWS BULLETIN!"

The young ladies stopped in their tracks. Everyone gathered around the box radio in the corner. The announcer started talking and the program came on by him saying,

108

"THE WORLD TODAY, brought to you by shortwave radio from our foreign correspondents overseas. Columbia brings to you the latest in World News. Sponsored to some of these stations by Golden Eagle Gasoline. Go ahead New York."
The New York announcer started talking as if he was in a complete panic! One could tell he was trying to keep control as he stated in his professional voice,

"Pearl Harbor, Hawaii has just been attacked by air, President Roosevelt has just announced. The attack has destroyed all Navy and Military operations on the principal island of O'ahu."

Lucy held her breath. This was so horrible! Sally's father looked as if he were in shock! He said in a repeating kind of way,

"The Japanese have just bombed our port in Hawaii."
They could not believe their ears. Pearl Harbor had just been bombed. The bulletin did not give many details, but everyone listening froze into the spot where they were standing. No one could believe the words that were coming out of that box radio. Lucy's thoughts ran wild as she thought,

"Oh Dear GOD, Pearl Harbor had just been bombed! What would this mean? In everyone's mind, the war was supposed to be in other countries. The United States owned Hawaii. The United States had stayed neutral up until now. What was happening? What was going to happen to America? What was going to happen to all of the boys who were stationed everywhere?"

Lucy's friend, being a teenager, was a little more carefree. She let it be known that she believed that the island just bombed still seemed so very far away. Although a very large tragedy, the war troubles seemed to be far away to this teenage friend. Lucy could not share her friend's thoughts. She panicked!

Often Lucy was way past her years in maturity. However, she had other reasons to be scared as well. Her uncle was in those islands, right now as they speak. Her thoughts also included her brothers. Would they have to go to war? She thought of all of the young men who would now end up in the heart of that terrible war. Lucy realized that her friend had not yet grasped the seriousness of the situation. Sally's parents, on the other hand, seemed very, very concerned! This only intensified Lucille's fears. The girls spoke only lightly about it as they left to go to Sally's room. Lucy was silently panicking. Since her friend was not taking it so seriously, she felt if she said anything about her concerns, then that may panic her friend. Lucy knew that she had every reason to be scared, but was too shocked to share her fear with her friend.

The Herms family had not lived alone in the not too distant past. Mrs. Herm's mother had died while she still had two little brothers at home. Mrs. Herm's had raised these boys. No one at their new church knew anything about this, because the young men no longer lived with the Herms. The older brother had married and now lived on a farm just north of the town that the Herms were living in. The youngest, Uncle Jordan, had joined the Navy. Lucy wrote to him just about every week. He was on a ship. Lucy panicked every time she thought of this,

"Yes, Dear God, Jordan was stationed in the Hawaiian Islands."

These two uncles were just the same as brothers to Lucille. She had just received a letter from Jordan at the end of this very week. He had told her that he only had one more year, plus three months left to serve. His last words on that letter were,

"I'll be home soon sweetie! That is if Hitler doesn't get us first."
Did he have a premonition? If he did, he was wrong, it was not Hitler. It was the Japanese.

J.R. returned to pick Lucille up about two hours later. He had not listened to any radio. Lucy began filling him in on what had happened. He got really quiet and the look on his face was that of complete shock. He became a white ashen color. After much delay, he said,

"Jordan will be okay Lucy. God will make sure of that."
By this time both of the young people were on the verge of crying. J.R. said,

"This will probably put the United States right in the middle of the war."
He remarked on how he had always felt it was just a matter of time, since the rest of the world was pretty much at war for a year or two by now. They both knew how very serious the recent bombing could be!

Upon their arrival home, the rest of the family was getting ready for church. J.R. and Lucy could tell from the minute they walked through the door that their parents already knew the tragic news. Mother had been crying. Her eyes were all swollen and red. Father nodded his head to the children as if to say be quiet. He then said in his ever so calm soothing voice,

"We will request prayer for your uncle tonight at church. Everything will be okay."

Their mother just looked at him with a look of begging. Her eyes were begging him to be correct! Mrs. Herms acted as if she wanted some sign from her husband that he knew this to be true. She knew her brother was on one of those ships, she could only pray that none of the ships bombed was the one Jordan was on.

Monday came and the Herms children went on to school as usual. At the lunch bell, Lucy and Sally grabbed their books and headed across the street to Sally's house. When they arrived, the radio was playing. Sally's family was sitting in chairs all around the radio. The president of the United States was speaking. He was announcing that the United States had just declared war upon Japan. J.R. had been so right! The United States was going to war. The President of the United States made an eight to ten minute speech. Lucy remembered one thing above everything else that he said. This statement had so much power behind his words as he said,

"December the seventh, nineteen and forty-one will be a date which will live in infamy!"

The whole afternoon was filled with talk of the war. Teachers had returned from lunch with radios in tow. Each school teacher tried to explain to their students their understanding of yesterdays events as much as they could. The seriousness was striking everyone's hearts as they learned of all the casualties. They learned of the massive amount of ships that had been struck. Many were sunk with men aboard. Lucy wondered if anyone else in her class could be waiting to hear about one of their loved ones. Could anyone else be wondering if their loved one was still alive? Each class had a radio playing with the news.

One teacher tried to teach her students about the islands. The students learned so much this day. They learned that Pearl Harbor is a harbor on the island of O'ahu, Hawaii. It is west of Honolulu. Much of the harbor and the surrounding lands were a United States Navy deep water naval base. It was also the headquarters of the United States Pacific Fleet. The attack on Pearl Harbor had been accomplished by the Empire of Japan. This happening on the Sunday past had brought the United States into, what would now be considered, World War II.

Lucy was so thankful the teachers had explained so much. She now had a better understanding of what was about to happen. Though quiet and shy, Lucy raised her hand and asked the teacher if anyone knew which ships had survivors and which ones did not. The teacher snapped her head around as her sharp eyes met Lucille's. She thought,

"Dear God, this child has someone close to her on one of those ships!"

Then the teacher looked at Lucy with so much sympathy. She had realized at that moment that this shy child must have someone in the danger zones. She shook her head as she said,

"No Sweetie, I don't."

She then asked the class to read a couple pages of their lessons. She went quietly back to Lucille's desk and asked if she was okay. She asked her, in a whisper,

"Who do you have in the service, dear?"

Lucille said,

"My uncle."

She then added,

"But he is more like a brother! My mother raised him along side of us."

Lucy could see the sympathy upon her teacher's face, but even that did not ease her pain. She was so frightened! Yes, Lucy was frightened! Very frightened indeed! She thanked the teacher and told her that she was scared and worried. The teacher asked,

"Would you like to be dismissed from school early today?"

Lucy told her,

"No Thanks!"

Stating,

"If I go home it will just be harder. My mother is falling apart!"

She also knew the worrying pain was going to be there no matter where she might go.

Within a couple of weeks, the initial shock wore off of the United States people. Mrs. Herms and her family waited patiently for any kind of word from Jordan. They started to become somewhat relieved after a little over a week. They had heard on the radio that the families of the casualties were being notified one by one. No one had come to see them, so maybe no news was good news. On Tuesday of the second week, a letter arrived from Jordan. Everyone leaped for joy. He had written his letter in great big letters across the top of the page, stating,

"I'M ALRIGHT! They got my ship, but I'M ALRIGHT!"

What a Heaven sent relief! Mother cried, Lucy cried, J.R. hugged his brothers and father said a 'Thank You' prayer to the Good Lord above.

Jordan's letter went on to say,

"I was topside and ashore. This caused me to be able to be rescued."

As if hesitating in his letter, he went on to say,

"I lost so many friends that day!"

He then ended his letter with a brief,

"I love you all and I will write more soon."

He stated of how one has to know of all the confusion and the work that has to be done at this time. Then in big letters again at the bottom of his letter he wrote,

"WE'RE AT WAR!"

J.R. had graduated High School the last school term. He was eligible for the service right now! About four weeks after the tragic Pearl Harbor bombing, he did get his papers. The Herms family became extremely frightened. J.R. seemed to accept his fate and chose to join the Marines.

One afternoon, shortly thereafter, as Lucille and her younger brothers came in from school they found J.R. sitting at the kitchen table. He had a big sling hanging down from his shoulder and a cast upon his arm. At first the siblings laughed at him. Their mother gave them a look that let them know this was no joke. That it was instead, very serious. They learned that J.R. and their father had been changing a tire on the car. The lug wrench slipped. J.R. did not let go of it fast enough and it had snapped his arm bone.

Their mother explained of how she could not imagine how this could have ever happened while his father was actually working with him. She mentioned all of those times the children had jumped down from hay lofts into stacks of hay. The times they would find a limber poplar tree and climb to the top of it, only to swing it almost to the ground. How it did not break, she would never know. She even brought up the time J.R. had been snake bitten by a copperhead snake. Yet, he had hobbled all the way to the house. This, he did while his leg was turning black all of the way up to his hip. She spoke as if she was giving an order,

"Injuries around this household are to be when you are playing! Not when you are working with your father!"

She was acting as though she was disgusted with her husband for letting such a thing happen. Lucy chuckled a little because she did not quite understand why her mother seemed so mad at her father. She knew her mother was very nervous about the whole ordeal. Mrs. Herms mumbled as she left the room,

"At least this might keep my son away from the battlefield a little while longer."

Lucy realized this was the whole reason for her mother's over reaction. She was also showing the true fashion of this family. She was trying, very hard, to see some good in everything. This poor woman was beside herself. She was so worried!

Chapter 11

Once again the hard winter came. Visiting with the older sister, for James Dahl, was far and in-between. The winter of 1941/1942 was extra cold. The Herm's family had a nice Christmas. J.R. had informed the marines of his broken arm and they had reported back to him that he did not have to report to the service until his arm was completely healed. Mrs. Herms was so relieved. The things she was hearing on the radio about the now World War II was scaring her to death. She had prayed daily for her brother and her son's safety.

The Dahl family also had a nice Christmas. Mabel had delivered a beautiful little baby girl on November 17, 1941. Her daddy and mommy were so very proud. Grandma Dahl could not have been happier. She and the sisters spent every minute they could making pretty little dresses for their precious angel. Uncle James fell in love with this beautiful little girl immediately. She smiled all of the time. Everyone would almost fight to get to hold her.

Mabel and Bryon still lived just across the field. The Dahl's owned many sheep and amongst them were several males. They owned only two bucks. The rest had been neutered, thus causing them to be wethers instead of bucks or rams.

Wethers are much less aggressive than bucks. The rams or bucks are very distinctive because of their large horns. Everyone knew the one ram or buck, as one would call it, was very aggressive. This animal was quick to anger. James and his brothers had jumped out of harms way with him on more than one occasion. In the month of February, during one of Mabel's walks to her mothers, the ram came up to her along her path. Mabel was carrying the three month old baby. The ram knocked her down. He then started to pound her with his large horns. She did everything in her power to protect her baby. Thank goodness it was very cold outside and she had dressed herself and her little girl quite warmly. If Mabel had not done this, and if they were not bundled so tightly they both could have received very serious injuries.

The timing was right, thank God, to where the boys were starting to do their chores. They heard Mabel's screams for help. If the family had been inside the house they would have never heard her. This was due to the proximity of where the ram attacked her. Everett panicked and screamed,

"GO GET HER!"

Dale and James took off running just as fast as they could go. When they arrived at the scene, the ram was gouging Mabel in the side with his large horns. He had used all of the force he had. The boys screamed as loud as they could but the ram would not stop. The minute they got right up to Mabel and the baby, Dale ran to Mabel while putting himself between his sister and the ram. James tackled the ram with all of the strength he could muster. That animal was very strong. It somehow got James to the ground twice.

Not knowing the seriousness of Mabel or the baby's injuries, James was panicking. He fought and fought with the crazed animal. Finally when it was all over, he realized he had used excessive force. He stopped just as he realized that maybe he had hurt the ram badly! He realized he was stomping the head of the animal into the ground. Mabel was sitting up by now and had been watching the massive fight. She screamed,

"We're okay James! Please don't kill him!"

James realized that due to his fear he had not known when to quit punishing the animal. While breathing harshly, James let the ram go from beneath his large foot. The now beaten animal; drug himself off into the outer part of the pasture.

James went to his sister to check on her. Dale was checking the baby's damages. He was disrobing the baby to be sure she was okay. Mabel had a big scratch under one eye and it looked as though she was going to have a big bruise around her mouth. She told her brothers that she believed she did not have any broken bones. She did tell them however, that her legs were shaking too much to get up from the cold ground. After checking little Carolyn, they found that she looked as if she had just tumbled with the blows and did not seem to be hurt at all. She had cried for awhile from the shock of what went on. When Dale Henderson picked her up from her mother's arms, she gave him one of her famous big smiles.

James did not even try to get his sister up to walk. He just swooped down and picked her up into those big arms and carried her all the way to the house. As Dale walked into the house carrying the baby, James came in after him. He kicked the door open wider to make room for him and his sister. Their mother went into one of her high fear panicked moods. She kept asking if maybe they should call the doctor. She undressed Carolyn again and looked her all over with what one would say, a fine toothed comb. She turned her upside down and she rolled her from side to side. The little girl laughed the whole time of the examination. So everyone assumed little Miss Carolyn must be A-Okay. Their mother started a thorough examination of her daughter, who in turn was reluctant all of the way. Mabel kept reiterating that she was fine! Her mother seemed to ignore her while she screamed to the others of how she wanted that crazy animal gone from the farm by sundown. Mabel kept saying,

"No mother! No, I'm fine! Carolyn is fine! We will just have to be more careful the next time. I will start carrying a big club. James just about killed the poor thing out there awhile ago. I will bet that ram will think twice before he attacks another human being."

It was decided to not worry Bryon just yet. So Mabel stayed for her visiting and then Dale took her home in the car. They would tell Bryon when she got home. Mabel was worried that he would not want her to walk across that field anymore. She also knew their mother would not give it up. By the end of Mabel's visit, their mother had decided they would sell the ram or just give it to someone. Of course they would warn the new owners of his mannerisms. He was not going to attack another family member of hers, never, ever again. So after much discussion, it was decided to get rid of the ram.

In the next few weeks the weather started to clear up some. After the wet spell, it would be time to plow the fields and get ready for planting. It had been too cold or too slick to even think of going to their older sister's home. She had not been able to come visit the family either. Now, the deep mud would prevent visits for another couple of months. This was the first Christmas Elizabeth had spent away from her mother and siblings. She had written and said they had a nice Christmas with just her, Mathew, Simon and Ruth. She described her tree and all of the gifts she had received or given. She had made a big beautiful card for her family. She had pasted pretty paper roses around it and had drawn a big Christmas tree in the middle of the front. This card was a much larger size than regular. She had placed a poem that their deceased sister Gwen had written. It was a poem about a Christmas past. Under the poem, she had written,

<u>**"Lest we forget!"**</u>

Being closer to their ages, everyone knew she was truly missing her lost siblings. The poem read as follows:

A SAD CHRISTMAS

Black was the night on Christmas
Not many years ago
Whilst the West winds fast were blowing
And the streets were white with snow

Through the window panes so clear
Shone the beautiful lights from the tree
And there were many spirit filled people
Whose hearts were filled with glee

You could see the merry makers
While they played, danced and sung
This Christmas was their happiest
For each year they had more fun

While many people were happy
With their Christmas joy
There came some poor ragged children
A poor ragged girl and boy

They went to the door of a mansion
Asking for something to eat
Something for their Christmas Dinner
For they neither had bread or meat
The girl with her tangled hair
Stringing down around her face
Was cold from the wind and snow
Could hardly tell her name was Grace

She had with her a little boy
Shabby and ragged were his clothes
And the pain the children suffered
No one ever knows

Their mother was sick at home
In her shabby little bed
With great holes in her cottage roof
Where they could see the stars overhead

They had no father
For years he had been dead
And their mother was afflicted
It was plain to see, they were not well fed

The hearts of the rich were not touched
Or did they give to the poor girl and boy

Then the children went to their mother at home
Their hearts were not filled with joy

They ate no Christmas dinner
But still filled with a heart of love
They left this cold world together
And went to their home above

Elizabeth had written on the back side of this card of how she felt this was her sister's dying message to all of her family. Elizabeth wrote,

"She wanted us to be sure everyone remembered those less fortunate than ourselves on this Christmas Day."

Then Elizabeth put a P.S. which said,

"I wonder what made her write such a poem."

Mabel remembered this poem well. She had written it down for her sister Gwen during the time period when she was too weak to write. Mabel had also wondered if maybe her sister had seen something like this while she was living in Columbus, Ohio. Or, she was possibly telling of other's sorrows so she would not have to dwell on her own illness and her upcoming untimely death? If she wrote it so that her family would not forget her, there was no way that could ever happen. How could anyone ever forget that their beloved sister had died one day before her twenty-first birthday, or that she had died of Tuberculosis? The family had always included the two siblings who had past in every event celebrated. They remembered them with each holiday. They especially remembered them on each and every Christmas. Remembering the two had made the things like the reading of this poem a Christmas family tradition.   Their brother, sister and father were all missed.

Even though it was now February, the family had left the beautiful card and poem upon the wall. As James walked by the poem, on this day with it's almost tragedy, he thought of how thankful he was that his sister Mabel and her daughter had not become victims today.   He wondered if there were maybe peep holes somewhere in Heaven to where their loved ones were looking over them.   Were these loved ones asking God to protect the remainder of their wonderful family? As James thought of the losses his poor family had endured, he could only hope that someone was watching over them.

Chapter 12

On the very first pretty weekend of the spring, James hoped into his Model T and bounced right over to his sister's home. He had missed everyone so much. Mother had a cold this weekend and was unable to join him on this journey. Bella and Edith had come along. Everyone was very happy to see each other. Elizabeth voiced her concerns about the fact her mother could not attend the visit. Her children looked like they had grown a foot a piece over the winter months.

The family attended the little church in the neighboring town that Sunday morning. James had gotten braver over the winter months. He had made plans and he knew exactly what he was going to do concerning his love life. Just as Lucille Herms came walking up the church steps, he stood right smack dab in front of her while blocking her way. He said,

"A top of the morning to you Miss Herms!" Before she could say a word, he asked,

"May I have the honor of asking if you would go on a date with me?"
He knew he should get this all out immediately before he lost his nerve. Yet he had a deadly fear that after so many months she could be seeing someone else and he may get a big **(NO)!**

James was tipping his hat to Lucy and smiling with a great big smile. She looked shocked at first, but she gave him a big beautiful smile in return. She said,

"Why Mr. Dahl, I would be most honored to accept."

James could have leaped sky high upon her acceptance. He quickly added,

"Of course I know this is contingent upon your father's approval."

She laughed wide eyed and said,

"Why, of course Mr. Dahl!"

James found he was now walking on air. He felt as if his feet were not touching the ground. Miss Lucille Herms had just made him the happiest man alive. Now, if he could manage to keep up his nerve while asking the very stern Reverend Herms. He looked around and he saw the minister talking to a group of men just outside the church. He waited patiently until the Reverend started into the church. He wanted to be sure the gentleman was all alone upon his approach. Just as the Reverend started up the steps, James ran to catch up with his pace. He wondered if sweat beads were showing upon his face. Too late now, he thought. He blurted out what he wanted to say very quickly, once again too fast with the fear of losing his nerve,

"Reverend, I know this may not be the time or the place, but I would like to ask you for your permission to date your daughter?"

The good Reverend Herms just glared at him through those steel blue eyes. He stared directly into his eyes for what seemed to be an eternity. Then, in his most professional voice, the Reverend said,

"Son, I love my daughter."

He just left that statement hanging out there in thin air. What else, if anything, was this scary man going to say? James could feel heat flowing up his spine. Suddenly his palms were soaking wet and his nerves were completely shot. He knew this man was toying with him. After much delay, James mustered up enough courage to say something else. As if in an answer to the statement that had been made much too long ago, James replied;

"Yes sir, I understand that!"

Then, after even more delay, the Reverend said,

"We have rules! We have schedules and curfews around our house! **Boy**! Do you think you could live up to that?"

Feeling this as some sort of an okay, James regained a little of his nerve as he looked the stern, stiffly dressed man straight into the eyes. He spoke as if answering an Army Sergeant,

"Yes Sir, I believe I could."

James reached out to shake the Reverend's hand. Just as the minister took his hand into his, James was not sure whether the man was going to shake his hand or knock him out. Slowly James could feel the grip of the older gentleman's hand and he heard him say,

"Well then, if my daughter wishes to date you, then you have my permission young man."

James could not remember how many times he said,

"Thank You, Thank You, Thank you!"

He just knew that he kept repeating it over and over again until he was starting to feel like a real idiot.

After the Reverend disappeared inside the large double church doors, James ran to catch up with Lucille. He told her that they now had her father's permission to go on a date. As he felt the blood coming back into his face, he then asked Lucille if he could sit with her in church. She agreed. He was so nervous. Even though this was of very little relief, James could tell Lucy was nervous too.

Lucy had a pretty handkerchief in her hands. It looked as if someone had crocheted the lace around it the very same color of her dress. She twisted this handkerchief as if she were trying to get water from it. Yet, every time James looked at her, she would smile. James could tell she must like him too. However, he was afraid to make that assumption prematurely. He was afraid these kinds of ideas may jinx him.

After church, James had to explain to Lucille that his sisters were along with him on this trip. But he explained that he would come alone the next Saturday night and the two of them could do something together. She replied with only a,

"Great"!

While giving him a pretty smile.

James said his goodbyes and then he seemed to just float out to his car. He felt like he was walking on air. He knew that he was! At this very minute, he was the happiest man alive.

During the car ride to his older sister Elizabeth's home, the two younger siblings would not quit teasing James. They laughed about how he finally was going to be with his dream girl. Then one or the other sister would lean over and say,

"She is your dream girl, isn't she Jamie? Answer us Jamie. She is your dream girl, isn't she?"

James kept driving with that big smile plastered all over his face. He supposed he did look like the cat that had just eaten the canary. He thought of how if he died right now they would never get that smile off his face. He had just accomplished something he never dreamed possible and he was very, very proud of himself at the moment.

During the time James and his sisters were having a wonderful meal and a nice Sunday afternoon at Elizabeth's home; the Herms were busy with their Sunday meal as well. Mrs. Herms brought up the subject of James George Dahl. She calmly said,

"Lucy, I saw you sitting with that Dahl boy this morning. Is there anything I should know?" Reverend Herms just starred over the table at Lucy. He looked away long enough to motion for J.R. to pass him the bread. Lucy saw her father was not going to help her out any in this situation. If anything, she could see he was enjoying this minute. She could see a twinkle in his eyes as she knew he was thinking,

"How is she going to get out of this one?" Others may believe her father to be stern and inflexible. She knew him to be a soft, wonderful, and loving father. He worshiped his lovely daughter and she knew it. Now he was glaring at her over his glasses. She glared right back at him with a dirty look. She started to tell her mother of how she and James were only friends and of how the seating arrangements just worked out that way this morning. Mrs. Herms was not buying one word when she said,

"I do think James Dahl is a very nice young man. He is a very handsome young man, But!" She lingered on the (But). Then she went on to say,

"Do you know about his family?" Lucy gave her mother a shocked look as she answered,

"No, Why?"

Lucy's mother began to tell her the whole tragic story. She told her of how the Dahl family had lost three members of their family to death in less than two years. She told of how James had lost his father when he was only ten. Within a year, one of his sisters and one of his brothers had both died. All of this had happened to this young man even before he had reached the age of twelve. Lucy looked bewildered. She did not say anything for a while. Then she said,

"How terrible mother! That poor, poor family. Poor James!"

She then looked shocked as her mother went on to say,

"I hear one could not find better people. I am told they are each and everyone quite wonderful. You know that Nash girl, Hazel? She married one of the brothers. The one they call Everett."

Then her mother said,

"Honey, our family has been very fortunate. We have always been a very happy and carefree family. I would hate to see you get mixed up with a family that is so filled with grief. That poor old mother looks like a bony shell of a human being. One can see so much pain on her face."

130

Mrs. Herms continued telling Lucy that the oldest sister, Elizabeth, was even older than she. She told the scenario of how if Lucy and James should become serious and then if by chance she would marry James, she would have a mother-in-law old enough to be her grandmother. The woman could be either Lucille's mother or her father's parent. Her mother, like an afterthought, repeated herself by saying,

"That woman would be more like a grandparent to you."

Lucy reminded her mother that James was only two years older than she and that Mrs. Dahl was his mother. Obviously he did not believe her to be too old to be his mother. She did, however, feel she was being a little curt, so she did tell her mother she understood her worries. She also reminded her mother that she knew the young man, James, seemed to be a very happy person. Lucy continued by saying,

"He's also very funny, mother!"

She really wanted her mother to know that she believed James to be more than cheerful. Lucille knew she must quiet her mother's fears because she knew in her heart that she had fallen very deeply for this young man. As of right now, she could care no less if his mother was one hundred and five years of age. But, realizing her mother was definitely concerned; she told her mother that she was very sorry about her worries.

As the conversation continued, Lucy got up more nerve. Lunch was over now and father had relaxed to the living room. The brothers had gone their separate ways. Lucy proceeded to tell her mother of how she really, really liked James. Even though the Reverend was in the other room, the whole time he was listening to their conversation. He realized Lucy was smittened by this young man. The quiet Reverend Herms spoke up from the other room just then and said,

"Josie, I have already told the young man he could come to visit Lucy. I guess I should have consulted with you first! I'm sorry!"
As his wife stuck her head around the door, he looked down as if ashamed of himself and he said,

"I hope this it is alright with you."
Mrs. Herms sort of shuck her head in disgust, but finally she did say it was okay. Lucy threw her arms around her mother and she hugged her. Mrs. Herms could see how disturbed Lucy seemed to be by her discontent. So she reluctantly spoke, as if she could be a little in favor of Mr. James. She said,

"Lucy, he certainly is a handsome young man!"
The subject was dropped and the women continued cleaning the kitchen.

The following week passed slowly for both James and for Lucille. Both of these young people could not wait until Saturday night. Finally the date arrived. James hurried as fast as he could with his chores around the farm. Everett laughed at him all day. In a rare serious moment, he did tell James not to worry about the evening chores. He told him that he and Dale Henderson would attend to his share of work. Even with that kind jester, Everett could not pass up the chance for one last joke. He said,

"I sure don't ever want to be known as someone who would stand in the way of LOVE!"
Dale chimed in with,

"Oh Heavens No, we sure don't want to do that!"

James could feel his face turning red. Paybacks are rough sometimes. James was most usually the one who would tease everyone else around the Dahl household. He would sometimes tease until they could not take it anymore.

At the Herms home, Lucy was worrying! She worried all the day long that maybe things may not be perfect. She cleaned and she mopped. Her mother told her the floors were already perfectly clean but Lucy wanted to be sure they shinned. She used a paste wax upon the floors. She then put on a pair of bobby socks and slide all over the floors to make them shine. Just as she felt everything was completely perfect and just as she was going to go get dressed, her brother Lewis came running through the back door. He was pulling an old toy wagon with their little brother Henry inside of it. The wheels had mud all over them. Lucy screamed at him. She had screamed so loudly to where their mother came running. Noticing the panic in her daughters eyes, her mother rushed the boys right back out the back door. This was not done before Lucy was steaming. When Mrs. Herms saw how upset her daughter was, she helped her quickly clean up the mess. Her mother then hugged her shaking daughter. She then realized that her daughter's nerves were surely on edge. Rubbing Lucy's hair from her face, her mother hugged her as she said,

"L-u-c-y, I can tell you are really crazy about this young man, but you have got to not let him drive you nuts! Take it slow, get to know him. See if he is someone you want to spend the rest of your life with. Don't run into this like it is the end of the world."

Lucy knew it was already too late. She had surely fallen in love with Mr. James Dahl a year ago when she first laid eyes upon him. She knew in her heart it was already way past the taking it slow idea of her mothers. She must confide in her mother. Who else would be better to share these feelings with? As she told her mother that she could think of hardly anything else but James anymore, tears started to well up in her eyes. She wondered if this was the pressure of what was to come or could it be happiness. She was not sure. Part of it could be the fear of not impressing this Mr. Dahl with her best efforts.

Lucy started opening up to her mother. She told of how she had prayed for a whole year now that James would ask her out. She told of how when he was near her, she was never quite sure she would be able to continue breathing. Now that he had asked her out, she stressed to her mother of how she wanted everything to be so perfect. Mrs. Herms felt a lump come up into her throat. This is far worse than she had thought. This was already very, very serious. If this young man felt the same, and from his actions she believed that he did, then she was going to lose her daughter to this one. They were already in love. Her mother breathed out a sigh as she realized she had best try to get to know her new son-in-law to be. She wiped a tear from her eye as she told her daughter that she somehow knew everything would work out perfectly. The mother felt a sinking feeling inside of her as she realized this was already way too serious to try to defeat now.

In the next county, James fluttered around like a chicken with the head cut off all day long. Dale Henderson passed by him once while he was standing in a doorway. It looked as if James wasn't really there in the face. His eyes looked miles away. Dale reached out and slid his brother aside as he walked into the kitchen. He then said,

"Lord, mother, James has it bad!"

His mother laughed and asked,

"Tell me Dale, just what is (IT)?"

To Dale's embarrassment, he said,

"I think he is (Love Sick) mother!"

His mother laughed as she told him,

"This is a good thing for me to hear, because I had thought he was possibly losing his mind!"

They all had a good laugh over that. This was still unbeknownst to James, even though he was within feet of their conversation. He was lost in his deep thoughts. He was still standing, very stiffly, in the doorway. While ignoring the bewildered young man, Mrs. Dahl said,

"I don't feel guilty about teasing him, he doesn't hear us anyway, but I feel guilty for talking about someone being afflicted. Even if it was done in a joking way!"

She told of how she knew love could do strange things to a young person like James. Then she teased Dale when she said,

"Dale you acted as badly before you got your first date with Cleo!"

She then walked over to where James was standing and moved her hand past his face a couple of times. She then said,

"Maybe not quite as bad! But bad!"

Mrs. Dahl stopped the joking when she started thinking of how awful it was for her sister who had a son who really was, as one would say, afflicted. He was not quite right.

Like so many things with their mother, Mrs. Dahl took advantage of every opportunity she got to correct her children. Dale was terrible about picking on this cousin. Mrs. Dahl took this time and advantage to shame her son for doing this. Dale would often pick fiercely on the lad. He would do this by having him repeat everything he said over and over again. The boy stuttered and for some odd reason, Dale Henderson got great fun out of picking on him. The cousin did not seem to mind these jesters. He actually seemed to enjoy the attention Dale gave him.

As Mrs. Dahl's mind left her comatose son while he stayed in his trance in that doorway; she did think of how everyone in her family really got along great. Actually, the cousin liked Dale the very best. He followed him around everywhere he went when they came to visit. Knowing how ornery her children were about teasing each other and their cousins, this troubled Dale's mother. She wasn't sure her children should do such a thing to a mixed up person, even if every bit of it was just in fun. Since the conversation had now taken on a more sinister path, Dale assured his mother that he loved playing games with his cousin. He asked his mother to listen the next time they were there. He wanted her to know that he loved his cousin and ask her to listen to how this cousin giggled every time he would do such things to him. Mrs. Dahl did know it was all definitely in fun. She knew she was more concerned because she could not help but secretly have wishes that her nephew was normal. She knew down deep that this was more than likely what troubled her the most.

As the family's attention turned back to James, they found out that the whole time he seemed to be in outer space; he was only trying to think of what he was going to wear for his big date. The family learned this only after much questioning. He had been in such deep thought that he had not noticed the world around him. He should have known better because this left the door open. Of course everyone teased and teased him shamelessly. Finally, in the end, he laughed with his family and he ended up picking out the clothes he wanted to wear. He chose his black pants; the ones that had cuffs on the bottom of them. He chose a starched white shirt that had holes for cuff links on it. He had second thoughts about that. He did not want to look too formal, but still wanted to look nice. Dale finally told him that without a jacket he would not look formal.

Lucy was at her house having the very same kind of problems. She and her mother were quite the seamstresses. They could make about anything. Last summer the two had joined forces and made the most beautiful dress for Lucille. It was of a yellow taffeta and it was covered with a lighter color yellow organdy. Lucy thought of how pretty that would be. The dress, with its wide taffeta belt, was so very beautiful. She then realized it was most probably too early in the year to wear such a thing. So, she decided not to wear that dress. She then racked her brain to remember everything she had worn at each time she had seen the charming Mr. James Dahl. She did not want to wear the same thing again. After much thought and after throwing everything she owned out upon her bed, she decided to wear a ruffled, off-white colored blouse and a short black skirt. This skirt had a real high waste band. She knew she looked nice in this and she knew that it showed off her tiny waistline. Now for the shoes; if she wore high heels, that would be too dressy. So what was she to wear?

Luckily the women of the Herms family both wore the very same shoe size. Lucy finally asked her mother if she could borrow a black wedged sole type shoe from her. Her mother was more than happy to help her daughter look her very best. So she loaned her the shoes. Lucy's mother helped her with her hair as well. They placed an off-white colored ribbon around the back part of the head while pulling the hair back and up ever so softly. This showed off Lucy's pretty little face and her long neck. She looked dressy, yet casual. She was finally satisfied. This was the very look she was looking for. Finally, she was pleased with the way she looked.

While traveling the miles to Danville, James took it easy. He had started early enough to where he decided it might be nice to not drive at his normal high speed this day. The thought of how awful it would be to have an accident and then never get the chance to have a date with Lucille Herms crossed his mind. He laughed as he thought of what a weird why of thinking!

James suddenly realized that even with his slower driving, he was getting there way too early, so he stopped by his sister Elizabeth's to say hello. One look at her baby brother and she told him that he looked gorgeous! She kissed him on the cheek and wished him all of the luck in the world in his quest to win Lucille Herms's affections. Just as he started to walk out of the door, Elizabeth asked him to wait. She then ran to her bedroom. She came back out with a bottle of cologne. It was Matthew's. She put a few drops under James's collar. She then said,

"There! Now brother of mine, I know she cannot resist you!"

James kissed his loving sister on the forehead and said,

"Thanks Sis, I love you!"

As he went out the door, Elizabeth knew of how very important this date was to her little brother. She had never seen him this way. She whispered quietly to herself.

"This girl is the one. I am so sure that this girl is the one!"

James got into his car arranging his pants so as not to wrinkle them. He drove slowly so as to arrive at the front door of the Herms household right on time. As he walked up the steps of the porch, he could feel his hands getting wet in the palms. He talked to himself while telling himself to please calm down. Mrs. Herms answered the door. She gave him a nice smile. She said,

"Come on in James, Lucy will be here in a minute."

He looked around the room and noticed there was no one else there. Not Reverend Herms, not J.R., not Lewis or their little brother. He supposed J.R. was on a date with Eve. As for the others they were probably still outside somewhere. He found that the lack of the Reverend Herms was most unnerving. James snapped back into reality when Mrs. Herms ask him if she could get him

something to drink. He smiled at her and said,
"No Thanks, I'm fine."
He knew he wasn't fine, he could feel his knees
buckling underneath him.

Mrs. Herms asked him to have a seat. He
felt that she had done this just in time because he
was sure his knees were knocking by now. He
was afraid she could hear them. He knew he had
better get his nerves in check. This was not his
first date by any means, so why was this date
causing him to react like this? No matter how
macho he tried to be, he knew the answer to that
question the very minute it crossed his mind. It
was because this young woman was his lifetime
dream. She was everything he had ever wanted!
She was so much more! He could not mess this
up! No, no, he could not mess this one up in any
way shape or form!

James looked around the pretty decorated
room. He noticed everything matched in pretty
bright colors.   There were throw pillows
everywhere. They were so soft. He had never
seen anything like them. They had little wheels of
material all over them and were made in really
bright cheerful colors. On the tables were arched
and starched stiff dollies. Someone in this
household crocheted, obviously. He looked up to
see a big picture of a beautiful young lady. This
picture was about a 10" x 14" in size. He thought
of how pretty the girl with the blonde hair was in
that picture. He had thought it to be a painting of
some sort. Then he looked again and realized it
was the beautiful Lucille. Now he did feel over-
whelmed. All of a sudden he started questioning
why would someone so beautiful be interested in
him? All sorts of doubts started crossing his mind

140

and all with the wrong timing because he could hear someone coming. He heard every step someone was taking down the stairs.

James looked up just as the good Reverend Herms walked into the room. This is not who he expected! He jumped up from his chair and said,

"Hello Sir, how are you?"

To his surprise, Reverend Herms looked at him and smiled. This is the very first time he had seen the man smile. With his firm face, he did not realize the man *could* smile. The Reverend asked James how he was and asked him about his mother. James could feel every nerve in his body shaking. He was somehow able to answer the questions, and to his own surprise, with a little dignity. They talked about his brother Everett and his wife Hazel. They talked about the Nash family. They talked of his sister Elizabeth and her family. They talked about everything except Lucille. This seemed to make James even more tense and nervous.

Finally, the casual looking Reverend Herms started asking James what his plans were in life. The Reverend talked of the plans he had always had for his children, especially the plans he had for his daughter. The main fact he seemed to want to get across to James was that he wanted his daughter to be very happy in her life to come. He told of how he wanted all of his children to live in a Christian home. He then asked James if Josie, the Reverend's wife, had offered him anything to eat or drink. James answered by saying,

"Yes Sir!"

Just as abruptly as he had walked in, James watched the girl's father walk out of the room. What a **Relief**! Total relief came over him. He was, however, surprised! He was surprised that in a home setting, Lucy's father was quite nice tonight. He seemed nothing like the stern gentleman who gripped his hand so hard on that very first meeting day. James had been so very afraid of this man. Well he still was, but with a little more comfort.

Just as James was taking in the rest of the parlor with his eyes and while he was getting his nerves to calm down once more, in walked the stunning Miss Herms. As she walked through the parlor door, she honestly took his breath away. He had never seen her in the dust of evening. She seemed way more beautiful than he had remembered her. For what seemed like forever, he felt as if he was glued to the couch. He finally came to his senses enough to stand up to greet the lovely lady. James could not have known that Lucy was a nervous wreck too, because she was doing such a good job of hiding it. She asked if she could get him something to eat or drink. He got enough ability about himself to say,

"Maybe later!"

Now what was he to talk about? The war was the main topic of the day; but that had to be way too depressing to discuss on a first date. So the first thing he said was,

"You look beautiful!"

She said,

"Thanks, so do you!"

Silence over took them until Lucy finally asked if James would like to go for a walk. He jumped for that chance. He felt it would be so much more comfortable than the feeling of being in someone's house like this. That was not to say that everyone wasn't completely cordial. Actually, he found he could really like the Herms family. Even her father, who had given him the impression of being stiff and unbending, had seemed overly friendly tonight.

The couple went on a very long walk. They walked all over the town of Danville. They were still walking when darkness set in. The moon was fairly bright this night. Thankfully this added to their comfortable walk. They should have brought along jackets because they were getting chilled. James wanted to pull Lucy close to him, but he knew this would not be appropriate on a first date. So he reached over and took her by the hand. After a good while, the couple started back towards the Herm's house. They were still holding hands. Both had worried so much about what they were going to talk about. This was an unfounded worry because they found they were able to talk about anything and everything. They joked about a house someone had painted black stripes upon. They talked of how the face of the moon looked crooked tonight. They talked about J.R. and Lucy's other siblings. They talked about everyone in the Dahl family. They just had fun! Lots and lots of fun!

Being the young people that they were, they decided to race back to the house. This was just in the fun of the evening, plus they knew this would keep them warm. They hit the porch in a fast run, while giggling all the way. Just as they got into the parlor, Mrs. Herms placed a tray with iced tea and muffins upon a little table near by. She got in on the fun and laughed with the youngsters. James was so right. This was a very jolly lady. He had known from the very start that he was going to like Mrs. Herms very well.

James asked the sweet little lady what time it was and she told him it was 10:30p.m. Gosh, this evening was over. Reverend Herms had informed him that Lucy's curfew was at 11:00pm. Where had the evening gone? It was over way too soon. Trying to make a good impression, James knew he best eat his muffin and prepare to leave. He told Lucy he had a wonderful time, she told him the same. As he stepped off the steps of the porch he looked back and said,

"See you in church in the morning."
She said,

"You know you will, and I will save you a seat."
With that, James walked out the door. Slowly he drove the three miles, or so, to his sister Elizabeth's home. He could not remember ever feeling this happy! This complete! He knew this was the beginning of something he would cherish all of his life.

Elizabeth had not only left the front door unlocked for James, she was sitting quietly over in a darkened corner of the room. She scared James as he tipped toed through the living room. She quietly asked,

"How did it go James?"
He was most happy to share the whole evening with his wonderful sister. She was very excited for him and was so happy everything went so well. She knew she could not sleep until she knew her baby brother was home. She also knew she had to hear the whole story. This was the common practice of the Dahl family. They were always there for each other.

Chapter 13

Summer had creeped upon everyone. The heavy planting had been done and now, other than the daily chores, the farm families could relax a little. They could have reunions, have picnics, drive around and visit with friends. James had spent every Saturday and Sunday ever since way back in March at his sister Elizabeth's. She had, by now, made him a private room in the upstairs of her home. She had felt this necessary due to his every Saturday night date with Lucille Herms. James was so thankful for this. He had also taken on double duties throughout the week so his brothers would cover for him on the weekends. The whole Dahl family knew this was getting very serious. As did the Herms family.

Lucy's uncle had been home one time for a visit. The government had let him leave the war on what one called a furlough. This most usually would have never happened during the war. In this case, the uncle had suffered from pneumonia and the service felt he needed a couple weeks of healing time. His family laughed when they told him that they were almost happy he got sick. James had got to meet this Uncle Jordan. He liked him very much. James learned Jordan was not Mrs. Herms's only brother. She had several brothers and sisters. The youngest two, which included Jordan, had been raised by Mrs. Herms after her mother's death. These two were Willard and Jordan. Willard was the older of the two and he was married. By this date, James had met that uncle since he and his wife lived on a farm close by. He really liked Lucy's family, at least every one of them he had met to date. James found most of Lucy's family to have wonderful senses of humor. They joked and laughed all of the time. He believed he had never met a family that was so much fun. Being a jokester himself, James fit in with this family most properly.

James had now attended a couple of Lucy's reunions and he had found all of the family members were very nice people. He really enjoyed her grandfather. The whole family was just as religious as his family, but then they had grandpa. Grandpa chewed tobacco. Grandpa played a fiddle. His life's work was farming and playing music for barn dances. One could not say this funny old man was religious. Lucy's Grandpa was double jointed all over and Lucy laughed at him. One might better say she laughed with him all the time. This was her mother's father and the father of the two uncles that were so close. The grandfather looked just like a rag doll when he walked. He was a tall lanky man who did not look that unlike Abraham Lincoln. The strangest thing about this man was that everything seemed to go in all directions when he walked. Not unattractive, just unusual. This tall, thin man could dance like no other. James was happy that this man could be so cheerful after all that he had been through. He had lost his children's mother to cancer when they were all very young. He had married again and all of the children had loved their stepmother, but then she died too. The old man just gave up after that and never married again. His family, of course, wished he would go to church more. They wanted him to change some of his, so called, sinful ways.

Lucy's family was so much more colorful than James. James's whole family, immediate and extended, seemed to walk the straight and the narrow in every way. Lucy's family, on the other hand, had some more worldly characters. Her other grandpa had lived with them up until he died. This was when Lucy was about five. That grandpa was the minister's father. Lucy told James the story that her father had told her when she was a little girl. Grandpa Herms had run away. Her father told her of how he remembered the day his daddy just walked off. He said he was small enough to stand behind his mother's apron as he watched his daddy walk down a long dirt path, only to never see him again.

Reverend Herms was never told why his father ran away. He had several brothers and sisters and remembered how his mother had to take in washes to take care of her young. She struggled much just to raise her family. Reverend Herms, being the youngest child had held great resentment against his father all through his childhood. Then one day after he had married, he and his brother Will were working at carpentry on a job they had taken in a nearby town. Someone on that job was surprised when they heard the young men's last name. Being of somewhat an unusual name, it caught a man's ear.

The man said,

"Boys, do you by any chance know an old man who worked on the railroad many years ago by the name William Herms?"

The young men looked at each other and did not know quite how to answer. The stranger kept talking to them even though he did not get an answer directly. The man was telling them of how he was from another state and had once worked on the railroad himself. He told of how there was this elderly gentleman over in West Virginia who did not have any family. This old man used to work on the railroad. He was now unable to do anything. Neighbors around that area had been feeding him. If it had not been for that he would have surely starved to death by now. He was sick and now he was homeless. The man then stated,

"I don't believe the old man can make it through another winter!"

The stranger felt the old man seemed to be without anyone to care whether he lived or died. The Herms boys hardly answered the gentleman. Will finally replied with a weak answer,

"He may be relation to us."

and both left it at that.

The good Reverend Herms was not a minister at that time and Will was not overly religious either. Although they both hoped this was not their father; they were pretty sure from the description that it was. The two young men concurred on the subject. Both were thinking of what to do. The worst side of them was saying let him die for what he has done to us and our mother. The better side of them knew they had to admit this was more than likely their father and something had to be done. After much hesitation, the brothers went back over to ask the stranger more questions. Then they knew, once the weekend came, they would have to take a long drive into the State of West Virginia.

When the Herms brothers finally found the old man, they knew straight away that this was their father. The old man was so happy to see his sons. He cried. The young men could not fight with that no matter what their emotions may have been. Both had discussed on the way of the trip of how each was going to give this old man a piece of their mind. That never happened. So, they brought their father home with them. They cleaned him up and decided he was to live with Lucy's dad.

From the very start, the young Mrs. Herms was very sweet to the old gentlemen. She fell in love with him. He had turned into such a kind old gentleman. No one could understand what could have happened years ago to make him run off and leave his family. No one was going to ask that question either. The boy's mother had always refused to tell them anything. Now, if their father wanted them to know, then they guessed he would tell them. Their mother was still alive and she surely was not talking.

Lucy's Grandma Herms lived until Lucy was about seven years old. Frankly no one understood why she acted so forgiving. She helped Lucy's mother tend to the old man Herms until the very day he died. It was plain to see she had obviously forgiven the old man years ago. Maybe she was just too Christian to hate him. It was also plain to see that she still loved him. No one could help but notice that the old man later appreciated his family so very much. You could see the grandfather and the grandmother adored their grandchildren.

Lucy told James she did not remember the day her grandfather died, but she remembered the wake at their house. She told of how even though she was quite young she could remember the old man and knew exactly what corner they had placed his casket. The telling of this story opened up a path for James to tell of his loved ones. He told her how awful it had been at his house during all of the deaths. Talking about these things seemed to bring the young couple closer together. They had now opened up their hearts to each other. There was no question, they were in love.

Chapter 14

The day came when J.R. had to leave for his duties in the war. He would be in training for several months. His family was praying the horrible war would be over before he had to face battle. Lucy was especially disturbed by her brother having to go to the service. She and he were less than two years apart in age and were very close. On the day he was to leave, it was all Lucy could do to not cry. She talked about every silly thing. His girlfriend, Eve was trying so hard not to cry as well. Unlike Lucy, Eve did not always win that battle. These girls were also very close. J.R.'s girlfriend and her sister were some of Lucy's best friends. They knew they would have to stick together through it all. Reverend Herms gathered everyone for prayer. He prayed that God would protect his loving son. Lucy could tell the whole family was scared. They were proud of their son and brother for serving their country, but they were very, very scared. This was such a terrible war.

An officer had come to pick J.R. up. As the car pulled out of the driveway, everyone waved. They waved until it was completely out of site. Lucy put her arm around Eve and they slowly walked into the house. Lucy knew she had to be the brave one. She started telling Eve of some silly story that had happened to her and her older brother. She told of how right after they moved to these southern Ohio hills, she and J.R. were out riding the roads one dark night just for something to do. They were trying to find every little road around their new home. Then, as a game, they were trying to see if they could find their way home. This was after going down each and every little dirt road or path they could find. She told of how just as they came around this one curve, something jumped out in front of them. It was not so much of a jump, but rather like something really large floated across the road right in front of them. Neither could figure out what it could have been. Then Lucy said,

"Eve, do you suppose that was a ghost"? Eve laughed and said,

"No, Silly!"

Then they both had a nice laugh. Lucy knew this was taking their minds off J.R. and his departure. Lucy cared very much for Eve. She knew if her brother made it through the war, he would come home and marry her wonderful friend. She knew she was going to like having Eve for a sister-in-law.

Many months passed. News came that J.R. had finished his training. Lucy wrote to him just about everyday. The family learned he was only stationed in the states for a brief time. He told them not to worry because the Good Lord was looking after him. Uncle Jordan had written about all of the gory details of this horrible war. He had used about every word to describe this bloody war. Many of his letters contained words like, violent, gruesome, brutal, fierce or horrific. These details made this family worry even more. Now they had two loved ones in the war to worry about. They prayed for their safety each and everyday. For many weeks no one received any kind of communication. Everyone was frantic! Finally when a letter did arrive, the letter told that on August 7, 1942, J.R. had landed on Guadalcanal. Everyone ran to grab a map. No one had any idea where this might be.

When James was around he comforted Lucy as much as he could, but that war made him a nervous wreck as well. The tragedies of this horrible war was hitting home for everyone. Almost every week you would hear about someone you knew and loved. These young men were being killed or injured. The world was in complete turmoil. This made young people at home feel guilty for being at home. They were almost afraid to show any happiness. In James and Lucy's case, they were overly concerned with the war. They were very worried about their family and friends. Yes, they felt guilty for any happiness, but they could not help but be happy with each other.

The couple was now talking about getting married. They talked about it all of the time anymore. They were trying to pick out a date to have their wedding. Lucy liked the idea of Valentine's Day. James wasn't sure he wanted to wait that long. They talked the dates over with their families. Everyone was happy they were waiting awhile. No big plans were made for a big wedding. The families felt the longer they waited the better they would know each other. The couple did not feel that way at all. They believed that they must have fallen in love the very first day they had met.

Winter got bad and the young couple's dates started getting far and in between. Both would mope around like their best friend had just died. Someone would remind them of all the couples who had been separated by the terrible war. Then both of them would feel guilty. Christmas came during a snow storm this year, so James could not be with Lucy. Elizabeth, knowing Lucy was going to be her new sister-in-law soon, had invited her to their house. She ask her to come right after the roads had cleared some. So, Lucy spent a Sunday afternoon with their family. She was fitting in quite well with the Dahl bunch. They all treated her like family already. J.R.'s girlfriend, Eve, had also spent a lot of time with the Herms. These visits with their future in-law families made them feel closer to their loved ones.

James and Lucille finally set a date for their wedding. They chose February 6th, 1943. This would be on a Saturday and the whole family, on both sides, would be able to attend. This was contingent on the weather, of course. Lucy was going to live in the Dahl household. James had made no plans to move out of his home. He was much needed on the farm. Everything was going to be just perfect, with the exception of the lack of J.R.'s attendance. He would be greatly missed.

The week before their wedding, the couple learned the law was changing. The following week there was going to be a five day waiting period before a couple could get married. These five days were to be after one got their marriage license. What a shame, they were hoping this would not dampen their plans. Lucy's father worked a regular job at this time, along with the

154

pastoring of his church. His church was a small country church that could not afford to pay him enough to keep his family up. He was working out of town the first two weeks of February. He would only be home for the week-ends. This was hard on him, as he had to prepare his sermons and try to be there for his congregational needs. He had to preach two sermons on Sunday. He then must be prepared to go out of town in the wee hours of Sunday night, or one should say Monday morning.

The wedding plans had been for Lucy's father to make it home early that Friday evening. He was to meet his wife, James and Lucille at the court house. He would need to be there to give permission and to get the marriage license signed. On that Friday evening, everyone waited at the court house. They were getting so very nervous. They feared Reverend Herms was not going to make it on time. Each person started worrying. The jolly Mrs. Herms was trying to tell the young couple it was not the end of the world. If Lucy's father could not get there in time, well then they would just have to reschedule their wedding date. She did not believe that to be such a problem. Both James and Lucille looked so disappointed. They knew with the new law coming up, if they had to postpone, it would be an even longer wait. Once they got the license they would have to wait that five days before they could get married. Who was to know what could happen even then with the hinder-some weather they had encountered this year. Then either way, Reverend Herms would have to be at the court house because he would have to give permission for Lucy to marry.

The lady behind the desk at the courthouse could hear all of this conversation and she started to feel sorry for the young couple. She spoke up and said,

"I'll tell you what I will do! I will keep the courthouse open a little longer than usual if you believe your father to be here shortly."

Lucy was so happy that she almost cried, but she secretly prayed that her father would soon show up.

The good Reverend Herms did show up within the next ten minutes. Lucy and her mother both hugged the lady and thanked her so much for waiting for Lucy's father.

So, the next day became total kayos as everyone planned a wedding. The wedding was going to be held in the Herms's parlor. It was to be held during the early afternoon. Of course the Reverend Herms was going to hold the ceremony. At about noon, it started to rain. Thankfully, the weather was not cold enough to do any damage. All of the guest should be able to attend. The entire Dahl family had shown up at Elizabeth's home early that morning. Their neighbors and Uncle Andy were going to take care of their chores. Extended members of their family and the neighbors were happy to do so on this joyous occasion.

All through the day, James and Lucy were both tense with anticipation. They managed to keep two different households in a total uproar. James was ironing and re-ironing everything. He would shave; then he would shave again. He wanted his face to be the smoothest it could be. His whole family was trying to help him, but mostly everyone just went around in circles.

Everett and Hazel got a big charge out of this. Secretly, they believed planning their wedding had to be harder. They had a big church wedding, but they would never mention that in all of this kayos! They just sat back and watched the circus! All in all everyone was in a wonderful mood and all were having fun during this before wedding time.

Lucy's mother was hunting for something blue. Eve was there to help. She was going to furnish the something borrowed. She would loan Lucy a brooch. Everyone was so excited! Reverend Herms knocked a couple of times upon the bedroom door because he wanted to talk with Lucy. Finally Eve and Josie left the room to give the Reverend the time he needed with his daughter. He came in carrying his Bible and he told his daughter the first thing he wanted to do was to have a prayer for her. They both knelt and held hands. Lucy's father began praying and thanking God for the short years he had been able to have with his beautiful daughter. He asked God to bless this union and to stay in his daughter's heart forever.

After the prayer, they stood up and Lucy's father reached out to hug his daughter. He just stood there for awhile holding her close. Lucy knew he was about to cry. She said,

"Daddy, there will always be two favorite men in my heart. James can never take your place, he will have a place all of his own. You will always have the very same spot that I call yours, forever!"

He swallowed hard, and then told his daughter of how he liked her young man and of how he felt that his faith in God would make their life a happy one.

Reverend Herms then told his daughter that he knew there would be grandchildren someday. He told of how he wanted her to be sure to raise those children in a Christian way. She agreed to everything her daddy said. The two sat a long time with their arms around each other. How do you explain joy and sadness all mixed in together? This is what Lucy was feeling. She would miss her daddy so much. Lucy was daddy's little girl. She knew that. She had so many wonderful memories of her wonderful daddy.

Lucy, realizing this meeting between father and daughter had now turned into a very sad meeting for her father, she started joking with him. She laughed about the times her mother would want him to correct her. Spankings were common place in 1930's and the 1940's. Lucy's father would take his little girl into a bedroom, shut the door then tell her to cry out as he slapped the pillow. This was all because he did not want to spank his little princess. This finally brought laughter to the man. He said,

"Well maybe it would have been different if I had more than one daughter."

He gave Lucille a big squeeze and told her he loved her. She kissed him on the cheek and said,

"I love you too Daddy!"

As he left the room, Lucy heard him say,

"Josie, she is all yours."

Chapter 15

The Wedding went beautifully. All family and friends joined afterwards for cake and ice cream. It was nice for all the family members to get acquainted. Eve stated many times of how she was missing J.R. Lucy told her that she missed him terribly as well and of how she wished he could have been there for her wedding. Everyone talked of how brave this young couple was to get married in such horrible times. James and Lucille heard someone say something like,

"They're getting married while this treacherous war is going on."

Someone made the remark that it was probably just a matter of time before James would also be called to that horrible war. Everyone was worried! The young couple knew this, but today they did not have a care in the world. They could only think of their life together.

The wedding was held in the early afternoon. Once the reception was over, everyone started home. Lucy was extremely nervous. She was happy, but very nervous. She was moving all of her clothing today. Everything she owed was going into another's home. Thoughts were rushing through her head. She loved James with every fiber she had within her body. She did, however, wonder how the move into a home with the other family members was going to be. She felt one comfort was going to be that the baby daughter, Bella, was almost exactly her age. She really liked her and if they continued to get along, this would be like having a sister. This was something Lucy never had. She was surrounded by uncles and brothers, but no sisters. She was starting to feel pings of loss when she looked at her brothers. She would miss them so terribly much. She knew she was going to do that without any question. It was so painful to leave her daddy. Her father idealized her and she knew she was very spoiled. Her mother too, she was not just a mother to her but she was her very best friend. She was going to miss all of the fun they had together.

Lucy's mother had talked with her daughter much about the Dahl family. She had been so worried about the fact there was so much sadness within that family. They had lost so many loved ones and this could only cause lots of stress to all of the family members. Everyone who had ever heard of this big family had so much sympathy for them. People would often say,

"Oh! That poor tragic family! Or do you know what happened to that family?"
So many people would say,

"I cannot see how on earth they could have carried on."
Lucy refused to let any of the negativity destroy any of her happiness. However, now that she was actually going to that home she was starting to feel the pressure of everything she had been told. Another thing her mother had been so worried about was the age difference between herself and

160

the other mother. She remembered her mother saying that the older Dahl daughter Elizabeth was about the same age as Lucy's mother. Actually a little older! Thus meaning Mrs. Dahl could have been Mrs. Herms's mother. Lucy knew that her mother only hoped that her daughter would fit in well with this very different kind of family.

The Herms family was young and usually very happy. Mrs. Herms was a jolly lady who laughed with her whole body. She laughed all of the time. She saw fun in everything! Lots of games and laughter surrounded the Herms family life. The only serious minded individual in this family was possibly their father. Even he got into some good fun ever so often.

In all honesty, now the Herms family was starting to feel pain. This horrible war was starting to stress them out. One could not enjoy life much when their loved ones were fighting in daily battles. But up until this point, their life had been pretty good. Yes, the depression was awful. There were many times the church or churches could not pay Reverend Herms. Often they would pay him by giving him food. This is what kept the family from starving. Reverend Herms was a wonderful carpenter and a cabinet maker but in these times no one could afford any of that kind of work.

All Christmas's during the depression, the Herms family did not even put up a tree. They felt what was the use? They had nothing to go under it. Rev. Herms always told his family to celebrate Christmas with the remembrance of Christ. So they often spent Christmas Eve reading the Christmas story in the Bible while saying prayers for their country. They knew they were not the only ones who were suffering. Many were less fortunate than they.

After the wedding, different members of the family and their friends started to leave. All of the Dahl's hugged Lucy and told her of how they wanted to welcome her into their family. The Dahl family had brought two other cars so James and Lucy would have the privacy of the Model T. Lucy's uncle and some friends had tied all kinds of stuff onto the back of their car. Eve and her family had made a big sign that announced,

"**JUST MARRIED**!"

Everyone had great fun creating this mess. All of the suitcases left with the other Dahl family members. Lucy's life at the Herms was over. Everything she owned had been packed and moved permanently to the other household. Mrs. Herms cried! Reverend Herms hugged his daughter as the cars pulled out of the driveway. Everyone had the remnants of rice upon their persons. What a mixture of emotions on this day. Everyone was *SO* happy, yet somewhat sad with the moving from one place to another.

As the journey began one would have thought they lived in a big city. All of the cars were blowing their horns loudly. Lights were flashing on and off. But once they left their family and friends, the night was dark. Everything was quiet as the Model T traveled along the curving roads. Lucy slide ever closer to her new husband and laid her head upon this shoulder. She was basking in the love they shared. Each was very quiet. Every once in awhile, James would lean his face over and kiss Lucy on the cheek. He would softly say,

"I love you Mrs. Dahl!"

Both were so very happy.

Lucy could feel the car slowing. They were pulling into the Dahl's driveway. She noticed there was only one other car in the driveway. It must be Dale Henderson's car. She noticed that Everett and his family had gone on home. James opened the car door for his new bride. As they arrived to the house, he picked up his petite little bride and carried her through the door. Oil lamps were burning everywhere. The senior Mrs. Dahl stood statuette in the pretty lace dress she had worn to the wedding. There was an oil lamp flickering on a small table beside of this lady. Lucy could not help but think of how beautiful this lady must have been in her younger days. She was still a beauty.

Mrs. Dahl reached out and hugged her new daughter-in-law and said,

"I want to welcome you, my child, into our home. It is now your home too. Please be comfortable and I hope you will enjoy living here. I do know of one thing, and that is that we are happy to have you, my new daughter."
She kissed her on the cheek and said,

"It has been a long day. I am going to bed. The others are already asleep, I believe. I will see you two in the morning. Enjoy your evening."
With those words the new mother-in-law headed for her bed.

Lucy looked around this charming cottage. It was a farm house, but it looked more like what she would consider a large cottage. She supposed that was because of the decorating. Everything looked of an antique nature. Lucy had been here only once before. She believes she may have been too shy to look around much on that visit. Tonight she was really seeing her new home. This is where she was to live with her handsome husband. One thing she could not help but notice was the cleanliness. Just like her home, this mother must be another cleaning lady. She laughed at her thoughts while thinking of how she would not get a break from any of that fanatical cleaning that she was so used to. She remembered they were all of the same belief. She chuckled as she remembered what she had heard so very often,

"Cleanness is next to Godliness! Was that phrase really in the bible?"
She questioned that and thought maybe she should look it up. Lucy smiled as she noticed the house looked as if everything sparkled in this beautiful lighting. She was used to electric lights. She would have to adjust to the oil lamps. She knew this was going to be a large adjustment. Right now she thought the oil lights were very beautiful.

The tables were covered with pretty lace or embroidered dollies. The home looked unlike the Herm's in many ways. Lucy's mother crocheted all of the time and had high stiff crocheted dollies all over the house. Lucy surmised that Mrs. Dahl was more of an embroiderer, because there were birds and flowers embroidered on everything.

A warm fire was blazing in a potbellied stove that was by a wall in a small seating room. The house felt toasty. It was very inviting. Lucy could feel all of her tense muscles relax. She was beginning to feel very comfortable in her new home. Her new sister-in-laws had stacked all of their gifts neatly upon a side table. On the very top, someone had made a very big lacy sign that said,

"Congratulations! Mr. and Mrs. Dahl!"

Lucy thought of how very sweet that was of everyone who did this. The kitchen table was covered with a lace tablecloth. James mentioned this was highly unusual. He stated that there was usually a red and white checked oilcloth adorning their big table. He smiled largely, and one could see he was very proud of his mother for doing everything so proper. In the middle of this table sat a nice paper flower arrangement. This brought the only sad bit of conversation during the whole evening. James looked Lucy in the eyes and said,

"I can not believe my mother got these out for me. My beautiful sister Gwen was so creative. She made this arrangement."

A sad look came over James's face as he added,

"I wish she, my dad and John could have been here for our wedding. I wish you could have met them all."

Lucy put her arms around her big strong husband and secretly thanked the Good Lord above for the soft, sweet heart this big man had within him.

Mrs. Dahl had made a wonderful chocolate pie. It had been cut and a ladle was awaiting usage. Two fine china plates were placed very neatly side by side. Lace napkins were folded and placed upon these plates. There was a note between the plates that said,

"Please enjoy your wedding night Mr. and Mrs. Dahl. You will find the victrola cranked and ready to play. Mabel brought over some really romantic records for your use."

Then it was signed,

"Lots of love, your mother and mother-in-law."

Two glasses were standing tall for the apple cider that the new mother-in-law had provided. Lucy

165

wondered how it could be chilled as no electric meant no refrigeration. Then she remembered, with a smile, that this was winter. The charming lady had planned ahead. She had placed the cider outside so it would be just right for the newly weds. Lucy was so amazed. To think her new family would go to all of this trouble to help her and her new husband celebrate their wedding night. You couldn't hear a pin drop in the house by now. The whole house seemed to be for James and Lucille tonight.

James and Lucy sat quietly at the kitchen table for a good while. They looked at each other over the sparkling oil lamp. They poured the cider and sipped on it for awhile. They then decided to wait to have the pie just before they went to bed. After about an hour of watching each others eyes dance and each telling the other 'I love you' many times, they decided to move to the parlor. Lucy liked this pretty room. The oil lights made it look so inviting. James put on a soft record and they sat down on the couch. For about another hour they gazed into each others eyes. James knew Lucy was nervous. He was too, so they needed this time to relax with just being together and in each other's arms. James said,

"Lucy, I would ask you to dance, but I do not know how."
She laughed and said,
"I know you are joking. I'm sure you know that there wasn't much dancing around my house either."
Finally, James said,
"Let's go have that pie. It has been a beautiful day. I'm an old married man now. You're an old married woman and I'm hungry!"

166

Lucy laughed. James then added,

"If you are planning on staying married to this character, I guess you might as well get used to the fact that I have to be up early in the morning. This farm doesn't stop the needs just because I got married."

Then he said,

"Besides you need to know where your bedroom is, do you not?"

She laughed and said,

"With you, I hope!"

They went back into the kitchen and ate their pie. Lucy took the plates and placed them in water and was ready to wash them when James said,

"They will still be there in the morning!"

He then walked over and placed a long passionate kiss upon Lucy's lips. He told her to go over by the upstairs door while he blew out all of the lamps. He did not want her to fall over anything. He proceeded to blow out all of the oil lamps. The big man then picked his new wife up again and carried her up the narrow steep steps. He laughed while they were climbing up the stairs and said,

"In the process of trying to make our wedding night elegant; it is probably a wonder my mother has not burned the house down. She has oil lamps lit everywhere. She even has these lit here in the upstairs."

Lucy had never been in the upstairs of this house and she was very thankful there were lights on everywhere. Actually she could remember very little of any part of this house. The trip she had made once before was for a family reunion. Most of that day was spent outside. When James dropped her down upon the bed, she looked around.

"My, my,"
she said.

"What a large upstairs!"
James said,

"Its all ours!"
Dale Henderson had agreed to take a daybed in the small room by the potbellied stove. He did this so that the couple could have the complete upstairs. He knew he would be leaving soon so this was not a large inconvenience for him.

Lucy noticed that getting up those stairs was the chore. The stairs were long and very, very steep. The stairway turned and then there was a large solid door at the bottom of the steps. Lucy joked of how if one fell down the steps, that door at the bottom would surely catch them before they reached the parlor. She liked these upstairs very well, mainly because she could feel the privacy. Now she was starting to get more comfortable. Her new mother-in-law had over done everything for Lucy's benefit, up here too. Lucy said,

"I hope your mother thinks I am still worth all of this after she has lived with me several months."
They both laughed and James said,

"My mother loves you. The whole family loves you. What's not to love about you, darling?"
With that he reached down and took off her high heels, then he said,

"What do you want to do now?"
Lucy looked at him with a shocked look. The jolly man broke out into a strong laughter. James was making her completely comfortable. She knew that is what he was trying to do.

Thoughts were rushing through Lucy's mind of how society was coming out of the

168

Victorian ages.   Women still talked of how intimacy was something more of enjoyment for the men. As they were climbing into the bed, she said quietly to herself,

"I will not be one of those women. I'm going to love having my husband's arms around me for the rest of my life. He has promised to keep me, protect me and love me for all time. I know he will do just that and I will always feel loved and needed in these great big wonderful arms."

Chapter 16

Lucy became more comfortable at the Dahl household as the days passed by. She was so very happy with her new husband. James was surely happy with her. He floated around as if he were on cloud nine. He would sing to Lucy all of the time. Both he and Lucy had nice singing voices so they had fun making up songs and singing back and forth. The early stage of the marriage was wonderful because James took Lucy with him every time he walked out of the door. Lucy felt guilty often because of the housework. She would always offer to help, but most usually was turned down. She had taken on the duties of cleaning the upstairs and washing James and her laundry. She always helped with dishes. Mrs. Dahl had a routine down so well to where she really did not need that much help. The sisters knew exactly what they were to do and everything ran very smoothly.

One day, James was plowing with the two old horses. He was singing his favorite song,

"Don't Sit Under The Apple Tree With Anyone Else But Me."

Lucy was sitting under one of the hickory nut trees. James would look over with each turn. He would stop his song, wink and say,

"I love you, Mrs. Dahl!"

James had worried about Lucille ever since he brought her home. He knew her family lived in a small town that was surrounded by country. He also knew before this church, she had always lived in some form of a town or city. He worried about the rough terrain of the rolling hill farm. James felt so very protective of his new bride. There was no need however! Lucy had grown up rough and tough. She had three brothers and two uncles whom she went on adventure trips with all of the time. She may have looked like a little China doll and as if she may break, but Miss Lucy was one tough little gal. James had not learned that yet.

Maybe it was her youth or a way of getting James to not worry so much, but Lucy played a trick on him that day. She ran and hid from him. She had no idea he would completely **panic**! While she was laughing, he was scared to death. He was so sure she had fallen into a hole somewhere upon the farm. Lucy realized very quickly that this was the wrong thing to do to this loving man. She apologized and promised to never pull a trick on him like that again.

Most days after that, Lucy would just tag along behind James and sometimes try to help him. Often James's sister Mabel would come to visit, since she lived so very close. Lucy liked her really well. She had also fallen very deeply in love with her daughter Carolyn. Lucy loved this little girl. She would beg to keep her overnight or to spend whole days with her. She knew this was how it would be someday when she and James had children of their own. With Mabel's heavy work load while she was trying to balance her time with both her family and her husband's family, she was more than happy to let Lucy keep Carolyn often.

Lucy learned quickly that Carolyn was not just a pretty baby, but that she smiled constantly. Lucy liked the times she had the baby all to herself. She would comb and put ribbons in the little girl's hair. She enjoyed sewing pretty little dresses for her when they had enough fabric. Feed sacks were usually of a pretty flowered or striped material. Often an adult dress would take either a whole sack or one and one-half. This meant there was often enough material left to make a pretty baby dress. When they could afford it, fabric was purchased to make nice little dresses for the little ones. James's mother was most thankful that Lucille could sew so well. Rebecca Dahl's mother-in-law had taught her to sew when she was alive, but she only sewed for the essentials. Lucy was an expert. She sewed and designed beautiful clothing. She would put pretty ruffles and bows on everything. Lucy's mother had taught her every technique of sewing, years ago. She made every stitch of clothing she wore upon her back. With this knowledge, Mrs. Dahl turned about all of the sewing over to her new daughter-in-law.

After about a year of marriage, Dale Henderson married and moved to Columbus, Ohio. Edith moved away about six months after that. Dale had purchased a home with an apartment on the third floor. Edith was to live in that apartment. She had taken an office position in that city. Now there were only two young ladies to help Mrs. Dahl, so Lucy began staying around the house more. About once a month, James and his mother would go to Gallipolis, Ohio to take care of their farm business. Usually Bella and Lucy did not go. The girls had become great friends by this time so they enjoyed this one day of the month that they had alone.

One would think on a farm and as busy as the Dahl's were, no one would find the time to get bored. They should not ever have to hunt for something to do. But then! The young ladies were always so full of energy. Bella and Lucy knew the trips to Gallipolis were whole day trips. Being somewhat young and adventurous, the two got a bright idea on this one day. An old female hog had just delivered baby pigs. With Lucy being able to sew quite well, and Bella learning to sew, the girls put their idea into action.

The girls decided to make a dress for a pig. They were discussing their designs as if they were creating an outfit for a Paris Fashion Show. Once they came up with the dress design, they decided to make a headdress with ribbons of some sort for the piglet's head. When their outfit was complete, they proceeded to the pigpen. This pigpen was large and very muddy. Needless to say the pig was filthy. Catching it was one heck of an experience. Neither expected that the catching of a pig would be so hard. Lucy fell down once. She was giggling the whole time. As she was coming back up, she grabbed onto Bella's dress. As Bella went down she said,

"Gee Thanks!"

The girls could hardly keep their minds on what they were doing because all they could do was giggle. By the time they caught the pig, they needed a bath worse than the pig. This was quite fun! Once the squalling piglet got to the house, the ladies proceeded to bathe her. They laughed so hard to where Bella said her sides were hurting. The kitchen was now a disaster. They knew they must hurry and clean everything up before James and mother got home.

Worrying about the mess did not deter the fun the young ladies were having. Neither had laughed that hard in their lives. Now the piglet even had a name! They named her Lily. Then they laughed at how she certainly did not smell like a lily. Lucy and Bella had to take turns holding the pig down while each cleaned up themselves. Finally their finished product was complete. They thought 'Miss Lily' was quite handsome! About the time they had completed their task, James and his mother walked through the door. Mrs. Dahl screamed and laughed loudly as she said,

"Now, I have seen it all!"
James could not believe his eyes. He was laughing so hard his whole body shook. He hugged his mother and said,

"See mother, I told you Lucy would make me a good wife. Look at all of her talents! She can even dress a pig. My, my, some man is surely going to get a good wife out of my sister as well! Maybe she should put her new found knowledge on a resume. I am sure a prospective employer would love to know she can dress a pig!"
He kept it going by saying,

"One thing is for certain, with these two around no animal need ever worry about not being dressed ever so properly."
The whole family laughed for the rest of the evening over this experience.

Chapter 17

Fall was here! The Dahl family usually made a trip to Circleville, Ohio for an old-fashioned camp meeting. This camp meeting was held in August of each year. It lasted for ten days. The younger people loved to go. The younger generation would stay the whole ten days. They would stay in dormitories. There were long dormitories all over the campus. It was always great fun to interact with other young people who came to stay. The grounds were also the college grounds. Bella was going to stay the whole ten days. The other members of the family were to go up for each weekend's services.

Being the first trip for the new Mrs. James Dahl, Lucy was surprised upon their arrival when they were greeted by most of the extended Dahl relatives. Everyone seemed to know about Bella and Lucy dressing that pig. Their guesses were that Mrs. Dahl had written about this experience in some of her letters. Lucy was just now meeting all of the family members. What were they to think of a wife who bathed and dressed a piglet? In reality this broke the ice. The teasing began and everyone had great fun!

The beautiful old campgrounds had been around since way before 1900. Everything, except the electric and the loud speakers, was close to the same as it was in the 1800's. Lucy had come from a different denomination and had not attended this particular camp before. She was, however, surprised that her family had never attended because it was only about twenty miles below Columbus, Ohio. Lucy and her family had lived most of her life in the middle or northern part of the state. Even being of a different denomination, this camp meeting had to be well known. Besides their faiths were the same. Lucy wondered why her parents had never wanted to attend. This place was huge!

The family had parked in a distant parking lot close to the cities large water tower and a railroad track that had several rows of tracks. Lucy knew the family knew their way around this large place, but she felt relief knowing she could look for the water tower and find their car if need be. As they started walking towards the place where they would have to check in, the many driveways and walkways were wide and long. Bella's luggage was getting heavy for everyone. She had not only brought her clothes, she had many blankets and quilts. Lucy questioned her and complained. Bella said,

"Lucy, my reason for bringing so many linens is that the dormitories are very cold at night. They do not have windows. They only have big board door covers that get propped up during the day by a big piece of wood. The dormitories are long and open all the way through. A person can almost freeze to death at times. These buildings are not heated!"

They walked for what seemed like forever. They passed one long two story building after

178

another. Every building was the length of an army barracks. That is what the buildings put you in the mind of, an army barracks. Even though Lucy had never seen an army barrack, she had seen pictures of them. Each of these buildings was called a dormitory. They had one that may have a (J) on it. This building may be for just boys and men. Then they may have another with a (M) on it and it may be for just girls and women. Then they would have some like (G) and (H) that had separate rooms where a couple may stay. All of these buildings were very plain. Though painted on the outside some years ago, each were made of only wood on the insides. No paint, no nothing, just the raw wood. In the middle of the private rooms was one lonely light bulb hanging down from the ceiling that was attached to its own cord. You either had to unscrew the light bulb to turn it off or use the strings attached to them.

When everyone was finally checked in and they had located their space, they walked with Bella to her far away dormitory. The teen or young ladies dormitories were back even further. One good thing about these buildings was the fact that there was a bath, of sorts, at both ends. These were furnished with a commode and a sink. Upon the property there were huge bath houses for both men and women. These had many showers and many stalls but it was rough to walk the distance at night. Having a sink and a commode at each end of one of these dormitories was great.

Once the women climbed the stairs to the dormitory where Bella would be staying, they were exhausted. Of course James could not go inside this dorm. Lucy noticed quickly why Bella had brought all of her own bed linens. Some girls were carrying in those they had gotten from the office. Lucy could not help but notice the comforters had to be fifty or one-hundred years old. The old dingy sheets looked as if they had been washed, but the comforters looked as if they had never seen water. They were all the same brown worn color. You could see hints of maybe a red here and there, but any colors they ever had was long gone by now.

Bella's dormitory was open all the way through, just as Bella had said. It was open from one end to the other. It looked so long with one bed after the other on each side of the long room. An aisle way ran down along the foot base of the beds. You could barely see the other end of this building. The only reason you could see today was the fact that someone had left the opposite door open and the light was shining through. Every so many feet there was a bed. Sometimes it would be a double bed, possibly for two girls. Others were single canvas like beds. As the women were making Bella's bed, she did find some of the camp's comforters that someone had left the campus without returning them to the office. Bella picked up two of them and put them onto her bed. Lucy frowned and went,

"UHU!"

Bella said,

"Don't worry Lucy, I brought several of my own to place on top of these. There is a meaning to my madness. The cool air comes straight through these canvases and you really freeze. If you fill your cot full of heavy comforters and then place them underneath you, it works more like a mattress."

Once the family had delivered their luggage to everyone's rooms they went to freshen up. James asked the women to meet him in front of the dinning hall. When everyone was finished and met up with James, it was about time for the afternoon service.

Lucy looked around and saw what she thought were thousands of people. What a big place this was. A large bell was ringing very loudly. She looked up and saw it was almost directly over their heads. Her high heeled shoes were sinking into a gravel like substance. She had seen a truck earlier that had a long sprayer on the back of it. It was spraying a substance that looked like a watered down tar or oil. She imagined this was to keep down the dust, but felt it was doing horrible things to her shoes. She was relieved when James said,

"Let's go in so we can get a good seat."
On this hot afternoon, James told Lucy he wished to sit about half way down and close to the large propped up windows on the side for ventilation.

As the family started into the tabernacle, Lucy was in total disbelief. She had never seen a bigger place in her entire life. The building was built as they built buildings in the 1800's. The very high ceilings were open and filled with large timbers that went in every direction. Big lights and huge speakers hung everywhere. The floor was concrete and it went down grade exactly like a theater. There were bench like seats with strong wood backs going everywhere. She figured there were probably ten to twenty rows of these benches going across the building. Each bench was probably twenty feet long. Then the stage or podium was so far away she felt they would not be able to see anything. As they descended down the wide aisles, she looked behind her to see a large birdhouse like room hanging high above. This small room held all of the microphone equipment. There were about five men sitting up there to operate all of this equipment.

Once they were close to the middle Lucy could tell, thankfully, that she would be able to see the podium. She felt sorry for anyone who was late or those who had to be in the back of this large building. She looked out of the windows that were also solid board doors. These were propped up by another large board, probably a two by four. As she looked out, she realized each of these windows was as large as a wall inside of someone's house. The building was built so the roof came further out to where it covered the concrete walkway that was an extension of the floor. These walkways were very wide. Since the Dahl family had come in on the first bell ring, Lucy could still look out of the huge windows. She noticed still more of those long dormitory buildings. She also noticed there was a smaller white building with the same kind of propped up board wall. It had a big sign that said, 'College Gift Shop'.

James had told Lucy that between services this evening he would take her through the college. It was a large brick building close to the end of the long dinning hall. The three story building faced another street. In front of the building was a large fountain that was used as a wishing well by many. James told Lucy that they would make a wish in that fountain.

The next bell rang and the music started to play. Lucy loved the pretty music. It was upbeat and done by complete professionals. There was a

182

complete band. There was a large piano, a large organ and several trumpet players. As of right now, the piano and the organ were the only things that were playing. Lucy knew her husband played the trumpet. He had played bits and pieces of songs for her before, but she was not prepared for what happened next. She had been so busy looking around that she only half way heard James say,

"I will see you in a little bit, and I love you."

She looked around and James had disappeared. People were crowding in and sliding his mother and sister ever closer to her on the edge of the bench. She put her purse down so she could save James his seat.

By now things were getting loud. People were gathering everywhere. It looked as if all of the seats were filled. Lucy soon realized the building was in fact full because people started to line up around the very large window like walls. People were now several layers thick. The breezes stopped. Lucy had never been anywhere where there were this many people. Bella, realizing this was Lucy's first trip leaned over and said,

"This is because it is a weekend. There are several thousand people who attend these meetings on the weekends."

All Lucy could do was to stay seated while shocked! She kept wondering where James had gone. If he had gone to the bathhouse, he had best hurry back. She did not know how long she could hold his seat open for him.

Now the bright lights were on and the music was getting louder. All of a sudden an announcer came upon the podium. He screamed,

"Welcome everyone to the afternoon service here at The Mount of Praise Campgrounds! We hope you will enjoy the service and we know you will be blessed."

With that he introduced another gentleman as the song leader. The song leader stepped up to the microphone. He then asked everyone to stand and told them to turn to their hymnals on page 153. Lucy noticed there were song books on the back of the next seat. Thankfully there was also a cardboard fan that she put to use immediately. The whole crowd started to sing. They continued this same practice through three songs. Lucy was really enjoying this but started wondering about James.

Once everyone was through with the songs, a minister stepped up and prayed for the service. Now it was time for the entertainment. One gentleman had a group of steel guitars. He had them stacked like stair steps. Lucy had never heard of anyone so talented. This man played, "Life Is like a Mountain Railroad."
You would have to believe you were on a train. He made the instruments sound exactly like a train, whistles and all. He sat down and the announcer came back up to introduce the next performer. Lucy almost fainted. It was none other than her handsome husband. She watched as he lifted that copper cornet up straight in front of his mouth. He began to play that beautiful instrument. He played so beautifully to where Lucy cried. Lucy had watched James take out this pretty instrument on different occasions but had never heard him play like this. She remembered the fancy carvings upon this horn. She knew it was James's pride and joy! This instrument was

shorter than his silver plated trumpet. She honestly did not know what the difference was between a cornet and a trumpet. She only knew that the difference in the ones that James owned was that the cornet was shorter than the trumpet. James had told her that the cornet was a three-valved brass instrument that was shaped like a compressed trumpet. Its tubing is more conical than a trumpet and it has a softer, warmer sound. Now she wondered just what she did not know. How did this wonderful man keep her from knowing he was an expert on these instruments!

First James played an upbeat gospel song. One Lucy had never heard. She assumed it was a newer song. Then he played 'Amazing Grace'. The crowd roared with cheers. She looked up to the podium and saw the perfect form of her wonderful husband. He would sometimes turn sideways. Lucy noticed how he curved his back as he played and of how he reached his cornet up towards the skies. His pretty black waving hair was blowing with the wind that was sweeping through the stage of the tabernacle. He had on a light colored suit today and he looked wonderful. Lucy could only think that he looked just like she would visualize the Angel Gabriel would look while blowing his horn.

After the initial shock, Lucy looked over to her in-laws. She worded silently,

"Did you guys know he was going to do this?"

Both her mother-in-law and Bella smiled and said,

"He wanted to surprise you!"

Lucy laughed and said,

"Well, he sure did!"

When James came back to his seat, he looked radiant. His big smile radiated. You could tell he was proud of what he had accomplished. People all around them, in all of the surrounding seats were reaching to shake his hand and they were telling him of how much they enjoyed his playing. One elderly lady wanted a hug and said,

"Young man, that was very beautiful, so very beautiful!"

As James slipped into his seat, he leaned over and kissed Lucy on the cheek. She was flabbergasted. She said,

"James, I had no idea you could play like that! It was so pretty!"

James replied by saying,

"Did you like it Honey?"

Lucy said,

"I sure did and it seems everyone else did as well. Gee, I am surprised I married such a talented man."

Then she threw in a question,

"Do you have anymore surprises for me?"

James only laughed and put his arm upon the back of the seat behind his pretty wife.

Camp was wonderful. Lucille could not remember having a better time. For dinner they decided to wait on the picnic items until tomorrow. They had plenty of ice and everything would still be fresh for tomorrow's lunch. The family decided to go to the dinning hall for dinner. After they had successfully pranced through the extremely long line, they found a table in the corner. Lucy was so surprised at the amount of people who came up to talk with James. 'Holly Cow', did he know everyone? She guessed he did.

He had been coming to this camp ground every year since he was really young.

After dinner, Mother Dahl and Bella went their separate ways. Mrs. Dahl went to a cabin that her other daughter Edith and some friends had rented. James took Lucy for a walk. They walked all through the college building. Then they went through the back of the campus. Here there were lines and lines of cabins. Cute little cabins. Many had flowers around them. This was almost impossible because each was built right up to the little dirt roads. The roads between these cabins were wide enough for one car and were made of dirt. Each little road had many cabins on each side of it. James told Lucy that one could purchase a lot and build a cabin. The lots were not much bigger than the cabins themselves. The cabin would have to be winterized so you could rent it to the college students during the school year. Lucy learned the cabins were the main living quarters for the students during the school year. Some dormitories were heated and were also used by the students, but cabins were their main housing. There were only a few dormitories that were winterized. Most of these buildings were only for the purpose of this camp meeting.

As the weekend passed, it was as if James and Lucille were on a honeymoon. All of the work at home was being completed by Everett and the other relatives. This weekend was complete comfort. Lucy was so happy to meet all of James's friends and his extended family members. This was such a wonderful weekend. Lucy did not want it to end. She knew it would have to and they would not being coming back to get Bella the following week. Next weekend was for Everett,

Hazel and their family trip to the camp meeting. Her mother-in-law would tag along once more and then the group would be bringing Bella home.

Sunday, the family attended the early morning services. Then they had lunch on the grounds behind the car. James had packed so many fresh tomatoes. Mother Dahl had brought along a large wedge of cheese that she had sliced and placed upon the ground tablecloth. The sandwiches were delicious. Edith and her friends had joined them. Dale and his new wife Cleo were there as well. It felt like the family was having a mini reunion. What a wonderful time was had by all.

Chapter 18

During the early 1940's the Herms and the Dahl families lived in fear of the war. Every young man had very mixed emotions. Each wanted to serve his country, but each did not want to leave their families to fend for themselves. Lucy's Uncle Jordan was still fighting. Her brother J.R. was right smack dab in the middle of everything. Lucy could not help but live in fear. Her biggest fear was that one day her husband would have to go to that terrible war.

As the bloody years of the war continued, the United States service men fought over many thousand square miles. Letters would arrive weekly from those loved ones in the war. James had finally received word on many of his cousins and loved ones. His brother Dale Henderson had trained for the war and was on ready alert should he be needed. As of this date nothing else had arrived in their mailbox asking for the services of James George.

It was hard to be happy during these times but James and Lucille enjoyed their love and their marriage. They were hoping for a child but it seemed that was not going to happen anytime in the near future. So much time had passed to where they became afraid they may be amongst the small hand full of people whose bodies do not allow the birth of a child.

Bella had graduated High School by now and was making plans to move to Columbus, Ohio. She would be living in the apartment owned by her brother and his wife. She would live with her sister Edith. Everyone was aware the sisters had missed each other terribly. Lucy would tease Bella of how she was only a temporary replacement of her sister. They would laugh and tell each other of how that did not matter because they would be sister-in-laws forever.

Lucy would get terribly homesick at times. They would visit her parents often in the summers, but during the winter months the visits were further apart. She had a little brother whom she idealized. She knew he was growing up without his big sister. It was always great fun when they were able to visit with the Herms family.

James now loved the Herms family as if it were his own. Being the only son-in-law, he would tell everyone he was the Reverend's favorite son-in-law. The Reverend would always chime in by saying,

"He is also my least liked!"

Everyone would have a good laugh. James and his great big sense of humor had been the turning point in his relationship with his father-in-law. It was not long before he was calling Lucy's parents Mom and Dad. The family had become very close by now. James, hardly knowing a father of his own, was thankful the Reverend Herms had started to consider him a son.

James knew his mother was a good cook, but he was sure Mrs. Herms was a great cook. His mother had always prepared large amounts of food quickly to serve her large family. Mrs. Herms would work with her food. She was more of what one might call a gourmet cook. Her angel food cakes had to be made with duck eggs. This caused them to be taller and fluffier than any other. Everything this woman fixed melted in one's mouth. James thoroughly enjoyed eating at his in-laws.

Finally, into the marriage a few years later, Lucy realized she *was* expecting. No one could have been happier. She and James began the conversation of boy or girl. James wanted a boy of course. Lucy was so attached to their niece, Carolyn, to where she could have nothing but a girl.

The pregnancy went well. Mrs. Dahl, the worrier, watched over her daughter-in-law with a ruling hand. Lucy could be too much of a child or a tomboy sometimes. Mrs. Dahl did not feel she needed to be tracing around in the fields along side of James so much. Lucy, believing she felt wonderful, would often get a little upset with Mrs. Dahl. She did of course know the elder lady was trying to protect her and knew that she had only her best interest at heart. Besides the Dahl family had been through some nerve racking pregnancies with Everett and Hazel. So, to keep from getting mad, Lucy would get a needle and a thread and go design something.

Once Lucy thought of the problems Hazel had, she would feel guilty for being so upset about being house penned. As she listened to her mother-in-law communicate with Hazel, this would make her feel all better about the strictness she had to endure. Besides Hazel was there many days a week while Everett worked in the fields.

Their mother-in-law was even more protective of her. She was expecting again and her baby was due at about the same time as Lucy's. At this point Lucy felt her child had better be a girl. She had made so many girly outfits for the new baby. It was reassuring to know that she and her sister-in-law had the odds of having two different sexes of children. So, if she had a boy, Hazel would probably have a girl. Therefore the girl's clothing would still have great usage.

World War II raged on. J.R. nor Jordan ever got to come home. The entire family stayed in a worried state of mind about their loved ones. This was the most devastating war. Thousands upon thousands of American young men had died. The worry over one's family could not have been healthy for any pregnant woman. Lucy often panicked when she did not receive a letter from one of the boys on a date she had expected one. Turns out the boys were fine and Lucy weathered the storms. She delivered a beautiful baby girl. James and Lucille's baby girl decided to come into this world on one of the bloodiest days of the war history. The day of the Battle of the Bulge!

On this very day, the Battle of the Bulge began. German forces, under the overall command of Field Marshal Rundstedt, launched an offensive strike within the Ardennes Forest. This was between Monschau and Trier. The strike was aimed at recapturing Antwerp. They were also hoping to split the British and American armies. The attacking force consisted of the 6th SS Panzer Army on the right and the 5th Panzer Army on the left. On the right and left flanks were the German 15th and 7th Armies. Our Allied Forces were definitely taken by surprise.

The initial assault targeted the line held by the US 5th and the 7th Corps, parts of US 1st Army, in the US 21st Army Group. All were a part of the Allied Expeditionary Force. A brief artillery brigade preceded this attack. German forces were successful on that first day. German forces did breach the American lines. To make things even worse, poor weather conditions prevented Allied ground attack aircraft from operating. During all of the confusion, English speaking German troops put on captured soldiers uniforms, used Allied equipment and posed as Americans or Englishmen. These groups were able to infiltrate from behind the American lines. This caused uncertainty amongst our men. Meanwhile, the US 3rd Army continued operations along the Saar River. What a tragic day in the war. Then although many miles away, and unaware of the war conditions, this day was the very day the precious little Dahl girl decided to be born.

What would this child's life be like after her beginnings? This child arrived on a day of many first happenings. Being born on the very day of the 'Battle of the Bulge', which was the last German offensive on the Western Front during the World War II could have not started this pretty little girl off correctly. This was also a day when more snow fell in the foothills of Ohio than one could remember. The doctor had arrived and left just in time to miss the three feet of snow. For days, no one could get in or out of the old country road. Lucy had such a hard delivery. Bella was frightened to the point to where she said she never wanted children. She did, however, fall head over heels in love with her new little niece.

James had gone to his Uncle Andy's, who had a crank and holler telephone, and had phoned Lucy's parents with the good news. In the days that followed, Lucille's mother was dying to see her first grandchild. She could not wait for the snow to melt. So, she complained and complained until Reverend Herms drove as far as he could. He knew he had to get this impatient grandmother to see her first grandchild. If for no other reason he needed to do this to save his own sanity. He was perfectly willing to wait to see his granddaughter when the snow melted some, but NO! His wife could not wait!

They drove as far as they could, then Mrs. Herms put newspapers in and around her shoes. She then placed her husband's large rubber boots upon her feet. The tiny four-foot, eleven-inch tall woman traced through the worst snow storm the country had ever seen. She walked the whole two miles of the dirt road that was impassible. Reverend Herms would have to leave and then come back to get Mrs. Herms after the snow had melted some. This worried him terribly, but he knew there was no way to stop the determined little lady. Many times Mrs. Herms was unable to know if she was in the road or over the fields. Many times, due to the large drifts, she would actually lose the dirt road, at which time a little fear would come over her. But, this lady was full of determination! Once she fell down into a drift clear up to her waist! It was that kind of snow! When she finally arrived at the Dahl farm, she was wet. She was cold and exhausted. Mrs. Dahl hurriedly got her out of her wet clothes and gathered things for her to wear. The forever worrier covered the tiny woman up with a big quilt. Though frozen and maybe even a little frost bitten, a big smile came over the little lady's face the minute her pretty little granddaughter was placed into her arms. The trip was so well worthwhile! Well worthwhile indeed!

Shortly after the birth of this baby girl, the USA decided they did need James. Everyone was so torn by this decision. James had always felt guilty that many of his relatives and friends had to do their duty for their country and he somehow got to stay home. At the same time, he was scared to death. There had been so many killed. What would his family do without him? He had the total responsibility of his mother, his wife and now his child.

When the date came for James to be tested he rode a train to Huntington, West Virginia. By the time he arrived he was a complete wreck. His nerves were not good anyway. He, like his mother, was a solid worrier. He worried about everything. Once they tested him, they decided he was too nervous for any service duty. He told them it was more or less his deadly fear for his family and maybe they should test him again. They told him they understood that. They also told him it was not just his nerves. They said they did not really want to take a farm man that did not have a father. They really did not want a man who is the last son at home to care for his mother. Then an older officer from behind another desk said,

"Then throw in a wife and a baby!"
The officer hesitated a minute, then said,

"Sorry son, we can't use you!"
James realized very quickly that the service really did not want him. He felt relieved, yet somehow

like he was not doing his duty. He had some kind of a guilt feeling. None the less, the army sent him home to his family and James never had to go off to war.

The weather cleared and winter finally ended. Spring was fun for everyone, especially now with the presence of the new babies. Mrs. Dahl completed most of the care for the little ones as Lucy and Hazel were needed for the chores in the fields. Summer was a time for the church homecomings and the family reunions. Everyone had great fun. James's brother Everett and his wife Hazel had delivered their little boy just a couple of weeks before James and Lucille's little girl. It was great fun to take pictures of the two little cousins. They fit just perfectly in an old rocking chair. The girls would take diapers and tie them around the baby's waist, then through the rails of the rocking chair, thus holding the baby's up in a sitting position. The babies would enjoy their seat for a long, long time. This summer was passing with the family truly enjoying each other.

World War II did finally end. It ended during August of that year. August was the time of the year for the wonderful Mount of Praise Camp Meeting. None of the Dahl family would be attending this year. This was a big break in the family tradition and the trip would be greatly missed. No one could take that chance! Polio was running rampant! The horrible disease was covering the nation. No one wanted to have their children in large crowds. This family had no idea when they would be able to return to their much loved outing.

By the end of the war, sixteen-million Americans had served in the war. Of that sixteen-million, four-hundred and six-thousand American Servicemen, many died. The tragedies were not only those who died, many were injured badly and would not function well for the remainder of their days. Even worse was the fact that the government was unable to bury, recover or identify approximately seventy-nine thousand servicemen. This included those buried with honor but buried as unknowns. It included those missing in action and those buried at sea. Amongst those buried with honor were the one-thousand, one-hundred sailors entombed in the USS Arizona left in the depths of Pearl Harbor. Lucy could not help but thank God on a regular basis for saving her wonderful Uncle Jordan from that final resting place. Everyone looked to the Heavens and thanked God that this was finally the end of a long and bloody six year war; a war that had been fought over many thousands of square miles.

Chapter 19

The war being over was a wonderful relief. Life started to get back to normal. If one could call it normal. Many friends came back from the war with a missing arm or a leg. This was devastating to know. As for the Dahl and the Herms family, thankfully they all came home with all of their limbs in tack. Some were suffering from lingering mental stress. How could they help but remember all of the terror? Bella had met and married a wonderful man. He had returned from the war not being able to sleep nights. Mabel's husband, who was a fairly quiet man, came home even quieter. On the Herms side, J.R. would wake up screaming sometimes. This kept his new wife Eve stressed and worried about him. The experiences were difficult on all who had fought and survived one of the worst wars in American history.

A couple of years passed. James and Lucille had another child. This time it was a boy. He was beautiful, of course. He had much darker hair than the girl, but both children had pretty curls all over their heads. Once again, Mrs. Dahl kept close watch over the children while Lucille tended to her duties on the farm with her husband.

Realizing farm revenue was not quite adequate during these times at keeping a growing family going, James pursued other financial avenues. Being a personable and a rather friendly young man, James found he could be a good salesman. He understood the needs of others. In the farm county in which he lived, there were very few people who had modern day, anything! The wheels started turning in James's mind as he tried to think of something that would make enough money to give his family what they needed.

Lucille wanted a home of her own. She wanted this so desperately. James had no funds to create this home. Finally after many nights of research, James ordered a sales catalog from 'The Sunray Stove Company'. He had read everything he could read about these stoves. He liked what he saw and sent in a request to become a distributor for this stove company. He was accepted. When the catalog arrived, it was about three inches thick. The pricing was hiding in the catalog numbers. This would make it easy to know the wholesale price.

Sunray Stoves were in existence for many years. Sunray manufactured a wide range of products from gas ranges to wood stoves. Sunray products had been produced by several companies, one such as Glenwood Range. This company was based in Delaware, Ohio. Being an Ohioan, James was easily offered a Sunray dealership. James chose to sell the gas range. He traveled to every farm house he could find within at least a fifty mile radius. He started selling stoves like hot cakes. Being the entrepreneur that Mr. Dahl was, caused him to realize he had a good thing going. Now that he had sold these stoves, he had to promise he would deliver the stoves and would hook the stoves up to propane gas. James had

200

done his homework well. He contacted the closest refinery and set up an account to purchase LP gas. The location of this refinery was in Ashland, Kentucky. They had distributors in different parts of Southern Ohio. One such was in Marietta, Ohio. This is the one he would use to pick up his gas tanks. He would return the empties and make this run almost weekly. He was fortunate in the fact that this company was also willing to work with him.

Now, Mr. James Dahl had a business. It grew fast. It actually grew into a very thriving business. He had to work both day and night, but he was off and running. Most homes in the area were still stuck in the turn of the century. Most people still had wood or coal cook stoves, so this revolutionary change was wonderful for the community. James decided to take this still one step further. Once his business started profiting, he had purchased a piece of land over in a small town that was just two miles from his farm. This was a town his forefathers had developed and he wanted a piece of it. The property was located upon a very busy thorough way and he knew anything placed there would most probably be successful.

By the early 1950's, James was building a new home. He was also building a store upon his new piece of property. He decided to have a furniture store. He felt this would go along well with his business. He already sold stoves, so why not more household items. The most important thing about this venture was that this would give him a showroom for his stoves. So, he built a large ramp to hold his LP Gas bottles and he built his store. James was becoming a very well known figure and a very well liked gentleman within his community. Before long he had built his business to the point of about six-hundred LP gas customers. Yet, he was able to keep the old farm going. By now, his brother Everett had moved to just outside the city limits of Columbus, Ohio. There, he had purchased a large dairy farm. So, James did not raise the kinds of crops they used to raise. However, he did his morning and evening chores the very same as he always had. Being a strong young man, the farm boy was finding he could do most anything he set his mind to.

James finished his home in 1953. By this time, the Dahl's had another child. A beautiful little girl. She too had pretty blonde curls and was the apple of her daddy's eye. Once the family moved into their new home, they found the grandmother was not happy about the move. With her bad health, there had been no choice but to move her along with the family. She longed for her farm home. She had lived there so many years to where she felt it was a part of her very existence. It hurt James to see his mother so unhappy. Shortly after the move, her health failed even more. It wasn't long after the move when James's mother took to her bed and she just never got up again.

Approximately a year after the move; James's mother moved in with her daughter Mabel. Luckily she lived on a farm close by. By this time, the Dahl children had decided to take turns caring for their mother. James would visit her daily. His mother would always worry about the trips to pick up LP gas. He would have to stop and see her after every trip. She had fears the truckload of tanks may explode while making the forty-five mile trip home after picking up the full tanks. The worry was unfounded and all trips went as scheduled.

A few years after moving into their new home, James's mother was now living at still another sibling's home. This home was over one-hundred miles away. So, the worry that bestowed the young Mrs. Dahl on one particular night did not have to be shared with the elderly lady. Lucille was thankful for that. She knew the older lady would have been beside herself.

James was scheduled to be home by about 7:30pm. This time would have been at the latest. More than likely he would be home for dinner. The time for dinner was most usually 5:30pm. On this night it got to be 7:30p.m. and then it got to 8:30p.m. and then 9:30p.m. Lucy was scared. She prayed as she looked out of the window. With every car that passed by, she was sure it was her husband. The children were staying up and watching for their daddy as well. To not worry the children so badly, Lucy said,

"A watch pot never boils!"
Inside, she was coming apart.

At about 10:45p.m., lights started coming from everywhere. It looked like a funeral procession or a car parade. Each car was coming over the hill very fast. To Lucy's surprise, they were all pulling into her parking lot in front of the store. What on earth could be going on? Finally when about fifteen cars got stopped, Lucy could see the big gas truck bringing up the rear. Her big husband jumped out of the truck and started to directing traffic. She could hear the jolly man screaming and laughing as he had each driver back their cars side by side at an angle. He was having them park these cars in a grassy spot just in front of his gas ramp. All Lucy could do was watch in amazement!

After all of the cars were stopped, James started to the house. Behind him were a whole group of young people. There were two young ladies amongst the group. All looked to be in their teens. James threw the front door wide open and said,

"Lucy, can you make some tea or something for my young friends to drink?"
With the large family, now the store, friends and church people, Lucy was usually very well prepared for guest. She cut up lemons and made some fresh lemonade while all of these young people seemed to be enjoying James's company. She could hear so much laughter coming from the other room. She could see her handsome husband throwing back his head and letting out that strong laughter. He was so wonderful, but what was she going to do with him. He does some of the oddest things at times. He was such a man-child. Yes that is what it was called, he was a man-child!

As Lucille took a tray of lemonade into the living room, there were people sitting everywhere. Some were on the floor with their legs crossed in front of them. Some were on the arms of the chairs, and some just everywhere. Everyone was laughing and the place was bussing with fun. It didn't take long for the frowns of worry to leave Lucy's face. James sat down in the middle of the floor, right in front of the kids. Of course there was no way their small children could sleep. Susie had been asleep a little earlier, but the noise had awakened her. The three year old daughter jumped up onto one of her father's legs, she was

happy to see her daddy. He gave her a big kiss
and said,

"How is Daddy's girl?"

He reached around her as he counted out money.
He gave each of the young people a certain
amount of money. As Lucy was taking the glasses
into the kitchen, James followed her and reached
on top of the refrigerator to get the Sunday school
bus or van keys. Just as he bent down to put a kiss
upon his wife, she said,

"Okay buster, what is this all about? What
is going on?"

He laughed and said,

"We now, Mrs. Dahl, are the proud owners
of a car lot!"

While Lucy stood there dumbfounded with her
mouth standing wide open, James bounced out of
the door. He looked back while saying,

"Come on kids!"

Lucy stood there for awhile wondering where he
could have found that many kids to drive for him.
Also wondering where he got all of those cars and
wondering why she did not act as the adult and put
her children to bed! WOW! What an experience!

A few nights later, Lucy's parents came to
visit. They now lived in Marion, Ohio which was
a good distance from Lucille. They had been to
the new home only a couple of times before.
Lucy's dad had spent a week with them while he
built her pretty kitchen cabinets, but her mother
had never stayed overnight. Lucy was proud to
show off her fairly new home. This evening she
had cooked a large dinner and was enjoying her
family. This house had a large furnace, but homes
did not have air-conditioning during these times.
This evening was pretty warm. Bugs seemed to be

everywhere. The large kitchen had a refrigerator and a chest freezer all on the wall of the door. In the middle of the floor were pretty yellow Formica and chrome table and chairs. Lucy had chosen dark red Formica for her cabinet tops. The walls were painted a soft yellow. The kitchen was a very cheerful 1950's modern kitchen. The table was set just right for tonight's dinner. Both outside doors had nice screen doors upon them. The doors were open. The screen kept out all of the bugs except for a little black something that was able to come through the tiny holes of the screens. Lucy was fighting these bugs and trying to keep them from her food when her father came in and said,

"Don't worry so much about those tiny gnats, honey. Everyone will just think they are pepper!"

Lucy had been so busy that she had not heard her parents come in. She hugged her daddy, then her mother and even with all the nerves of trying to be perfect, she knew this would be a wonderful evening.

As the family sat down to eat. The Reverend said the blessing and everyone acted as though they were waiting on the other to say something. Lucy spoke up first. She told them that James would have to explain all of those cars out there. The Reverend laughed so hard he could hardly eat when James said so matter of fact,

"I was driving along when I saw a small car lot. I noticed they had a coke machine. I dug through the truck for change. I wanted a soda. An older gentleman came out when I stopped. The poor old fellow could hardly walk. I asked him about the four 1950 Fords he had on the lot.

Those pretty black cars had caught my eye. The owner took it to mean that I was interested in buying one of them. He tried a hard sales pitch. We talked and I found the old man was hoping to retire. So, having a lot of extra cash upon me that I always take for the gas pick-up, I made him an offer and to my surprise, he took it."

Lucy asked for the first time,

"Where did you get all of those young people to drive the cars home for you?"

She guessed she had forgotten to ask the next day, then life got in the way of thinking about it. James said,

"You know Eve's brother lives in Rutland? I knocked on his door and ask him if he could round me up someone to help. He called his Sunday school class and every one of them came to help."

The Reverend Herms laughed as he said,

"Now that is a match made in Heaven! We all know Eve's brother tries everything there is to try! You two should get along great!"

Everyone had a good laugh.

It was true! Eve's brother did try about everything. Eve's brother also had an LP gas route in a neighboring county. He also had a furniture store that was much larger and more successful. However the brother was not the only one close to James who was not afraid to try anything. James had a cousin who had lived on the next farm up the road from James when they were growing up. He had always tried everything to make money as well. When he was a child, he had taken a bushel basket full of old corn cobs and took them around to the farm houses to sell them for a nickel a basket. To everyone's surprise, he had sold all of them. The mothers always believed this was because he was cute, but time had shown he was quite a salesman. He now owned a very large, new car sales dealership in still another county. Then still another cousin who now lived around the Canton area had started what he called a soap box derby on the week-ends. He told James of how he would put big barrels out at the end of the road and ask attendees to donate money to the cause. He claimed he was making money hand over fist. This must have been true, because each year he would stop by James's house to see him on his way to Daytona Beach, Florida where he would take a grown up man's race car to race. Each year he had a bigger and a more expensive race car. It wasn't long before his little soap box derby race became quite well known as well. So, these boys must have had something inside of them that made them want to succeed. Or maybe it was just the times after such a depression and a war the world had to contend with. Whatever it was, these men seemed to have what it took to become successful.

The father-in-law joked when he said,

"I guess you are taking after Eve's brother and your cousins."

The older man laughed and then said,

"Lucy, what on earth are you going to do with your husband?"

You could tell the father-in-law was proud of his son-in-law as he said,

"I wish you all of the success in the world, son!"

Lucy did not know when it happened but she was happy that her father seemed to be completely fascinated with his son-in-law. She noticed that her father was very proud to be James's father-in-law. Her mother had told her as much. She told her that her Dad would often say,

"I could not have chosen a better man for our daughter than the one she chose for herself. He would always add,

"We are so fortunate in that respect!"

The Herms youngest son, Henry, had now married a beautiful girl from Kentucky and they had a daughter very close in age to the Dahl's little girl, Susie. The couple had come along on this visit. The little girls always had great fun together. Henry, finding that his brother-in-law now had a car lot, decided to buy a car. What else could one expect? He wanted one of those 1950 black Fords. All of the black Ford cars looked alike. How could you pick one? These cars were hotrods of sort and this family loved speed. Why wouldn't Henry want one of those cars?

The cars had big engines and were of a very sporty model. Since Henry and his family had ridden with his parents, it was easy for him to drive his new car home. He could see no reason why any of the family would think that unfathomable!

Henry told James not to sell the other two cars to anyone else before he spoke with his brothers. He was sure they would want one as well. Of course James had already kept one for himself. Every day some young man would stop and ask about those cars. James would rather his brother-in-laws have them, if possible. Before anyone knew it, James had sold all of the cars on the lot with the exception of the black 1950 Fords. He had received word that (yes) all of his brother-in-laws wanted one.

In the mid summer all of Lucy's siblings came to visit and to pick up their cars. They all lived in Marion, Ohio by now. The good Reverend Herms had been pastoring a church known as the First Church of Marion for many years now. This was a very large church and the family had settled in quite nicely within a large old parsonage that looked like an old castle. They had lived there several years now and everything was blessed with this family. All of the boys had married and lived close to their parents. This trip of about one-hundred and sixty miles was to be a vacation for all. The family always got together for a week or two in the summer. Since their sister stayed in the hills, their vacations were often spent with her. Often James and Lucille would join her family at Lake Erie where everyone would camp out for a week. That was their other vacation spot. The Herms were great campers! Poor Joyce, Henry's wife could never rest and enjoy her vacations. Everyone loved her biscuits too much and she had to make them wherever they went.

On this summer vacation, the Herms family was going to play with their new cars. The only other plan they had made was to make a trip to West Virginia. They were going way back into the state. No one had ever been there before. Reverend Herms had a much older brother who had married a West Virginia woman in his youth. He had moved to somewhere way back in the mountains. No one had seen this uncle in many years. Lucy and her siblings had never met him. The parents were to join Lucy, James and her brothers the following weekend. The entire family was to go in search of this brother of their father! Someone had given the boys directions on how to

210

get there. So plans were made to go visit this elderly gentleman.

It was always great fun when either side of the families came to visit, but the Herms boys were kind of younger acting and were so full of mischief. They kept everyone hopping. One of the very first nights of their visit with their sister, they decided they would go frog gigging! No one knew one thing about this. They just wanted to do it. James told them he thought they were all nuts and he would not be joining them. He said he had something better to do that night, and that was called sleep.

Someone had an old rowboat and off the young men went for their wild adventure. They spent their night on Raccoon Creek. The following morning the children and the sister-in-laws woke up to the loudest screaming and carrying on they had ever heard. This noise was going on in the Dahl kitchen. Lucille had attempted to please her wonderful brothers by cooking their frog legs. She knew nothing about how to cook them, but decided to put them in a skillet and fry them. To her surprise, the legs got up and danced out of the skillet. They then danced all over her stove. Although this food was suppose to be very delicious, no one got to try this delicacy on this morning. It was too much fun watching Lucy catch those legs popping all over her kitchen. Once she caught one, she would throw it in the trash can. The men nearly died laughing at her. James and his brother-in-laws were having a blast. Each one of them had taken a chair around the table. They all rocked back on their chairs and just watched with sheep eating grins upon their face. They each stated they did not know when they had laughed that hard. They were getting such a large charge out of Lucy's demise. Henry threw his arms up behind his head and would sometimes say,

"There's one Lucy, you'd better catch it!" Lucy was now doing some kind of a dance herself as she was hopping around the legs that had danced off of her stove and onto the floor. She pretended to be mad at her brothers, when in reality she had not had that much fun in years. This sort of thing was not unusual about her brothers. Not so unusual about her husband either, as a matter of fact. In Lucy's eyes, he had become more and more like her brothers as the years went by. But she realized he had always been on the mischievous side himself. Everyone was crazy and having tons of fun this week. She was so happy to have these wonderful brothers visit her.

As the weekend approached the family was getting ready for their trip. All the young men started up the 1950 Fords. They left them running for what seemed like forever. Eve was outside with J.R and asked why they would do such a thing. J. R. laughed and said,

"It's just a man thing!" The pretty dark headed woman came back into the house with a puzzled look upon her face. She looked at her sister-in-laws and said,

"I'll never understand any of them. They are wasting gas. Lucy, your husband is as bad as the Herms boys. They are all hopeless!"

The next time the girls looked out of the window, they saw Lewis hooking up a water hose and marching it down towards the cars. The cars were all four lined up, side by side, neatly in a row in the store parking lot. Eve said,

212

"They just washed those cars this morning. Watch those idiots! I think they have lost their minds! I've got to see what this is all about!"

Giggling and running to see, all of the young ladies gathered in front of the large picture window. Lucy had organdy crisscross curtains on the window. They had to pull the curtains back to get a better look. The pretty women stood there in wonderment. No one said a word. Eve and Lucy both had their hands over their mouths. They looked as if they were in shock as the men, one by one, crawled under their cars with the water hose. The cars were still running. In a few minutes the ladies could hear the cars get louder and louder. All of a sudden, it was sounding as if a freight train was coming straight through the living room. What on earth was going on?

As the ladies held their hands over their ears, finally the cars got shut off. Just as school boys, the young men came bouncing into the house all full of laughter and mischief. No one understood, but they were proud of what they had just accomplished. The women did not know what that was, but they could see much pride upon their husband's faces. Yes, these young men had accomplished something their wives could not understand. For a few seconds the girls just starred in disbelief. Then Lucy spoke up first as she ask,

"Would someone like to tell us what the devil is going on and what was that all about? Did you idiots just blow up your engines?"
James replied with a big smile,

"No, doll face, we just busted the glass!"
Eve screamed,

"WHAT!"

The guys knew she believed they were talking about the glass windows. They got a charge out of her dismay. Each of these fellows loved to tease. Their wives knew as much and most usually they tried to protect themselves from being the butt end of a joke. But today, not one woman knew what these guys were talking about!

J.R. laughed and said,

"No, No, the glass that is in our tail pipes, silly! The tail pipes are glass pipe mufflers. That means they are lined with glass. If you want them to be loud and go Da-a-a-a-a-a! Then this is what you do! You get the tail pipes very hot; then you run cold water over them, thus breaking the glass that is concealed inside of them!"

Lucy replied with something like she now was sure they were all completely nuts! Neither Lucy, nor Eve was convinced. The other ladies were smiling and acted as though everything was quite normal with their young men's actions. One guesses these guys do so many crazy things to where these women are used to whatever happens with their carrying on. Of course Eve and Lucy were the little bit older ones and maybe they were trying to be a little more rational. Maybe even more sensible!

Eve spoke up this time and said,

"What do you mean THAT IS WHAT YOU DO? Are you telling me these cars come with instructions that one should get the car **really, really** hot, then try to tear it up by putting cold water on it?"

Eve was showing signs of really getting upset. Lucy was not too happy either. If their sister-in-laws had no problems with this, then they just had not been around long enough to think about

214

wastefulness.   You know the throwing money down the tube type deals.   They too will see someday! Eve did not wait for the answer to her question. She left the room with a huffy statement of,

"You guys will never grow up! You will just never grow up!"

Lucy   understood   her   sister-in-law's frustrations. Everyone except Lewis had children by now. Funds were hard to come by and Eve was feeling the pressure of what she believed to be J.R.'s wastefulness.   James took Lucy aside to calm her down. He whispered,

"This will not hurt the cars in anyway. It just makes them noisier!"

Henry reached over Lucy's head to the top of the refrigerator to get a ball that he called a suicide ball. She dodged down as she gave him a dirty look. The item was neatly packaged. It had an explanation on it telling that it was to be attached to one's steering wheel. It had a half naked woman's picture upon the ball and Henry was so very proud of it. James laughed at Henry while turning his attention to his wife. He suggested that she should maybe go and explain to her sister-in-law that the breaking of the glass would not harm the cars in anyway. Lucy shook her head in disgust as she went to do just that. After a brief time, everyone could hear laughter coming from the bedroom. They could hear Eve say,

"I still believe they are all nuts!"

Eventually   the   girls   came   out   of   the bedroom and started to pack the things they needed for their trip. All seemed to be well by this point. Oh, you could still hear chatter amongst them.   Sometimes they would laugh, other times they would complain, but all in all they accepted the fact that their husbands were far from grown up. With this bunch, growing up may never happen!

Chapter 20

The large family was ready for their trip to West Virginia. After all of the packing and the loading of the children, they selected where and how to get the family into their four black 1950 Fords. Once this was accomplished, they took off for the mountains. The Reverend and Mrs. Herms had gotten in the back seat of Lewis's car. Lewis having no children to date, this was the best place for them to ride.

No one had been on this trip before unless it was the Reverend Herms. What seemed like a comfortable family outing was starting to get dangerous! At least the women were starting to believe this.

There had been talks of the government building new and better highways. To date there was nothing but narrow paved roads passing up and down the mountains. It seemed the family had not gone very far once they crossed the Ohio River before the roads began to be very curvy. There were many curves that were called hair pen curves. The road signs would show a drawing that made the road look as if it came back and met itself. All of this was while you were very high up on top of a mountain. You could look straight down. Each woman was showing fear. The men, on the other hand, were having a ball. The lead car would zoom around a curve while the next car would follow almost upon the bumper. These men could drive very well, but they were driving way too fast for these curves.

J. R. had taken the lead. Lewis was second. James was third and Henry was bringing up the rear. The sounds of these loud cars were surely waking up the dead in this neighboring state. Lucy knew her brothers and husband were having much fun. She tried to enjoy the trip as well and tried to dismiss her fears, but she had to admit to herself that she was becoming quite scared. These guys did really know how to drive and they were racing through these mountains with great finesse! Lucy tried to come to grips with herself and she tried to laugh with her husband as he enjoyed this road trip.

Laugher came to a sudden halt just as the parade of cars circled one large curve. The car in front of Lucy and James looked like it was about to stand up on two wheels. Just as it came back to the ground, the left door flew open. Lucy could see her brother and her father's arms reaching out as they caught the door. Lucy's face had now turned white. James reached over and pulled her closer to him as if in a hug. But, not one of the cars slowed down.

Finally, half of the trip was coming close to an end. The cars started through a thick wooded area. This was nothing different than they had seen all day except they were now on an even narrower road. This one was dirt! All of a sudden, the first car splashed tons of water. It had gone into a creek. Once again all of the women screamed while believing everyone was going to drown. Once more the men had been up to their teasing and had not told the women about the need to ford a creek. So, with all of the windows still open, each car proceeded through that creek. Everyone in each car screamed. Everyone in each car was being sprayed with water.

Once glasses were wiped and eyes were focused, they knew that they were at their destination. Everyone was jumping out of the four cars and the women started pounding their hands upon their husband's chests. One of the girls said,

"That wasn't funny!"
One of the guys said,

"Oh yes it was!"
Even the serious Reverend Herms was laughing fiercely.

Lucy noticed they were in such a heavily wooded area. She told the others to watch for snakes. She asked the children to all stay very close together.

There were people sitting in the small cleared area. Right in the middle of this area stood a small rustic house. The siding was of a plank up and down. It was of a brown, rotten looking wood. Between each plank was another narrow board. Lucy imagined this was to keep out the weather. The roof on this small house had been tin at one time. Oh, it was still tin but she could not imagine how it kept out the rain or the snow. It was one solid piece of rust.

Lucy could not help but notice that none of the people, who were sitting around the yard, had moved. She noticed they did not seem the least bit concerned with this large group of loud people and their loud cars. This bunch was acting as though this occurrence had happened everyday in their wooded homeland. They did not even act curious!

One old, old man was sitting in a rocking chair. He had on bib overalls and had a large walking stick leaning up against his chair. Now maybe he had an excuse to not greet his guest, but what was with the others? Lucy assumed that this was her Uncle Jim. She knew her father had not seen his oldest brother for decades. Obviously, the elder gentleman had no idea that the Reverend Herms was his brother.

Once everyone got their composure back, they formed sort of a line as they started to walk up towards the house. Reverend Herms was leading the way. Now the elder gentleman was up on the edge of his seat. He said,

"Howdy! Can I help you?"

The Reverend Herms said,

"You sure can if your name is James Herms!"

Now, the older man rose and looked Lucy's father up and down. Then you could see tears forming in his eyes as he reached out and grabbed his baby brother, while placing a big kiss upon his cheek. He hugged him tightly and thanked him over and over for coming to visit.

Everyone was introduced to everyone else and all took seats that were scattered about the yard. No one went inside. Lucy guessed they were not invited in because the place was only a room or so big. She was somehow relieved because she was not so sure of what they may find inside anyway. Believing her uneasiness over cleanliness had to come from her being a whole German, she scolded herself for her thoughts. Then she chuckled to herself as she thought being German must not have anything to do with anything. Her uncle would, of course, be German too and everyone in that yard would be at least half German. She wondered at her silly thoughts. But none the less, she was keeping a very close watch over her children.

The day ended with the entire family being happy they came. Lucy saw tears in her father's eyes as they were leaving. She knew that her father believed this would be the last time he would ever see his brother.

The Reverend gathered his composure as the family was getting back into those four black Fords. He said in a loud voice,

"Alright boys, I know you had a lot of fun coming over here. I also know you scared the girls and your mother half to death. It will be getting dark soon and I am telling you to take it easier on the way home. You don't know these roads. Let us all stay safe. Remember the women and the children, Okay?"

Then he added in a stern voice,

"That was not a request. That was an order, boys!"

With that little lecture, everyone loaded up and headed home.

Lucy always enjoyed visits from her side of the family. They were too far and in between. James and his family were together most all of the time. Lucy's family lived further away and had become more distant. Her father had pastored the First Church of Marion now for several years. They had moved back to the Northern part of the state shortly after James and Lucille had married. She often teased her parents by saying,

"Sure, you only moved to Southern Ohio to get rid of me! Once I married, you moved straight back north!"

This night, Lucy was feeling the pains of her family leaving tomorrow. She knew it would be months before she would see them again. Now there was talk about her parents moving to Florida. Her father had become very ill recently. He had an exploratory operation to his stomach. The doctors had found a large ulcer. They had removed a large part of his stomach by now. He could not eat properly or anything. He was on a strict diet of baby food. He almost died. Lucy's mother was so worried about him and was feeling the large church, with the large congregation, was maybe too much for him to handle anymore. So in all probability, the older couple would more than likely move to Florida soon.

Lucy let her mind wonder as the group of cars headed through the mountains. Everyone was driving carefully now. The children were asleep in the back seat. Lucy knew James thought she was asleep as well. She was happy to have him believe that, because she was thinking about her life and her family. She loved her life, but could not ever shake the need to see her family more. Now, it would be even worse with longer extensions between visits. She had enjoyed this visit, so very much!

Chapter 21

The new week started off as usual. James was working hard each and everyday with his gas route. Lucy had a thought of how she sometimes hated their phone. Customers were to call once they turned their regulator over to the second tank. This was when they were to order new gas, however many would not call until the last tank was empty. Then it was always an emergency.

Today, James had taken their youngest daughter with him on his route. He did this often. Lucy could not help but wonder what she was to do to keep her girls as ladies. Their daddy was forever trying to make tomboys out of them. He had trained the oldest daughter to drive tractors and trucks when she was but nine.

Lucy knew some of her stress was probably brought on by the fact that she was more than likely expecting again. She had not told James this yet, but she had a very big feeling that she was going to have another baby. A few months ago she and her oldest daughter had moved some furniture. Lucy was of the habit of changing out her furniture whenever the whim arrived. The furniture store was so handy. James sold used furniture the same as he did new, so when Lucy got tired of a piece of furniture, she would go down to their store and find a piece she would prefer. She believed she had been expecting at that time. She felt awful afterwards and bled for days. She was afraid that she had a miscarriage.

Now Lucy believed she was expecting again. She knew things often happen after losing a baby. She knew she was going to have to take it easier around the house. Just the day before, she and James had gotten into a scuffle. James was carrying a bucket that needed water in it. He had reached high over the back porch to hand the bucket to Lucy. He asked her if she would please fill it for him in the kitchen. She had to make room for the bucket because she was in the process of washing dishes; therefore she took longer than James's anticipated. He screamed,

"Where is that water?

One time would not have been too big of a deal but by the time Lucy had filled the bucket, he had repeated his question three times,

"Where is the water?

Lucy being somewhat uneasy or maybe a little mad at the third question, thought to herself,

"I'll give you your water Mr.!"

So-o-o-o, she politely went over to the banister of their very high porch and dumped the bucket of water straight down over the top of her husband's head. Lucy knew the minute that water bounced over those large shoulders that she was in deep, deep trouble. She could hear the hose being attached to the faucet outside of the house. James was getting his own water. Great, that is a relief, she thought. Well, it was until she heard the back screen door slam. He was not taking the water to the chickens. He was coming into the house with it for some reason. Lucy took a worried look over her shoulder and ran straight out the front door. James was so fast that he caught the screen door right behind her. She ran down the steps and down the sidewalk. She started to gain speed as she darted between the store and the house. She did not look back so she wasn't sure where James had gone. All she knew was that she had out run him. But, he had out smarted her! At the very minute when she turned to go around the back of the store, James had gone the opposite direction. She screamed when she turned the corner because James was ready and waiting for her. He poured the whole bucket of water all over her. She thought,

"I deserved that and now it is over!"

The minute she could see, she started to run again. Due to the water in her eyes, she once again did not realize where James had gone. So, just as she turned to go back around the house, James got her again with another bucket of water. Finally they were both exhausted. The two sit down upon the front steps. James took his beautiful bride, water soaked and all, into his arms and told her,

"Don't ever try anything like that with me again. You know I'm bigger, stronger, and faster! I will always win!"

On those steps, that day, they had a good laugh as they often did over good fun things. As everything calmed down, the feeling of someone watching them was overwhelming. So, they turned to see their children's little faces pasted to that large picture window. Lucy said,

"Do you think maybe they are worried about Mommy and Daddy?"

James chuckled and said,

"They probably think we're crazy, but one thing is certain, they will never grow up believing that Daddy and Mommy did not love one another!"

With that they kissed and decided they needed to go clean up.

Lucy realized now that if they were expecting another child, they would need to calm down a little and quit some of their childish ways. Thank God, James had fixed the back step. One year ago, Lucy had stepped onto the top step and it came loose, thus causing her to fall. She had ripped her leg on a large nail. They had rushed her to the hospital where she had to have seventy some stitches. Lucy thought about that for awhile and realized that maybe they did play too rough. They could have been hurt with their water battle the other day.

School would be starting soon. Summer was coming to an end. Mrs. Dahl, James's mother, was not doing well. The family would be scheduling another trip to Columbus, Ohio before school started. Lucy felt this was a good thing because she could shop for school clothes at the Lazarus Department Store. This store had really good deals in their basement sales departments. James and Lucille had purchased all of their children's winter coats there for several years now.

After all of that water wasting, the weather had become very dry this year. The well was drying up some. This well was only used for drinking water and to do the dishes. The cistern was their main source of water. Without rain, the cistern was becoming very dry as well.

James had found a solution to their water problems. He would load up a wagon full of cream cans. These cans were those that had been left over from the days of much milking. He now used the cans to fill with water from the pond that was over on the old Dahl farm home place. He would take his Ford tractor; hitch it up to the flat wagon and load the cream cans. He would then go to the farm and head down the steep hill to the pond.

James always took his children along. On this one fall day he had his older two children with him, a girl and a boy. After he had filled all of the cans with water he had started back up the long steep hill. On this day, he had a very frightful experience. The tractor was loud and he was shocked he was even able to hear a child's scream. His son was screaming his lungs out! He was screaming hysterically! Somehow, James did hear the little boy's screams. He stopped the tractor, jumped down only to find his daughter's little head just inches away from the wheel of the trailer. She had fallen off and was about to be ran over. James got her up safely and put her on the tractor. As he jumped upon the tractor, he hugged his children ever so tightly. He raised his head to the Heavens and thanked his God for saving his child's life.

James moved his children to the large finders of the tractor where he could keep an eye upon them and he gradually continued his journey. On the way home, he debated as to whether to tell their mother. This incident had scared the youngsters so badly. He was sure they would blurt it out the minute they arrived home.

James felt like an old rung out dishrag as he and the children walked into the house. His nerves had gotten so tense with the close call to where he felt weakened. He knew he must tell Lucille immediately. He went straight to the kitchen where she was fixing dinner and put his arms around her. He told of the almost accident. Lucy fell into his arms and cried. She actually bawled. James just stood there and held her. He knew this was tragic, but did not expect that kind of reaction from his wife. She was not the one who was there and experienced the death rendering screams. She was not the one there who pulled their precious little daughter from the jaws of death. However he did feel very sorry for his wife at this point.

Lucille finished dinner and tried to analyze herself. She knew she had over reacted. She knew she had made James feel even worse for letting such a thing happen. He had sunk very deeply into his large chair in the living room and had not moved since his return. She knew he needed to unload the water and dump it into the cistern. Now Lucy knew that she had made her husband feel like the most irresponsible person alive. What was going on with her? Oh, she now knew the answer to that question! She was definitely pregnant! She knew that tonight she must tell James. She would feed the children and put them to bed then she and James were going to have a nice talk.

Finally everyone had eaten. The little bit of water left in the cistern had been used to boil water for bathes. The children were now fed and clean. They were ready for bed. The oldest daughter had complained about a toothache. Lucy had heated some water and put it into the hot-water-bottle. She had taken a towel and wrapped it around the bottle. Hopefully the little one could sleep. Her teeth were not good anyway, but her fall to the ground this afternoon had more than likely caused one of them to loosen and to hurt even worse. Lucy kissed her children goodnight and started into the living room. She knew what she must do.

James was sitting in his chair. He was all relaxed by now. He had a magazine in his hands. Lucy walked over and sat down upon the large arm of his chair. She leaned over and kissed her husband upon the forehead. His pretty blue eyes mellowed as he said,

"What did I do to deserve that?"
She said,

"Because you are wonderful and I love you!"
They hugged for awhile and neither said a thing. Lucy finally said in a soft voice,

"James, do you remember of how we talked when we first got married about how many children we wanted?"
James said,

"Yes!"
Lucy went on by saying,

"Remember you laughed and said you wanted nine just like your mother? Then you said no, you would never put me through all of that!"
By now James's eyes were dancing. He had such a wonderful sense of humor. He looked at Lucy mischievously and said,

"Okay, I don't know where you are going with this, but I do remember we decided to have four children, like your mother. We decided on that because that was a nice even number and we felt that would be the perfect family! Right? I'm forgetful. How many do we have now?"
Lucy laughed and thought of how amazing it was that her husband could bring her out of the darkest

moments with laughter and fun. He was so gentle and loving. He was just wonderful in everyway. How was she so lucky to find one as wonderful as he? She honestly believed there was no one else like him in the world. He often joked to that fact by saying that God had broken the mold when he made him. All joking aside, she often believed this to be true!

James had a stronger grip upon his wife by now as he said,

"Hey, have you noticed we only have three children? They are all asleep right now. How would you like to go and try to make number four? Maybe right now?"

He continued to tease her as he said,

"What do you say pretty lady? Would you like to try for number four?"

Lucy loosened his grip as she said,

"Please be serious for a minute. I have something very serious to tell you. You may not like what I have to say, so please listen carefully!"

James got quiet and looked his wife directly in the face as she said,

"James, I *AM* expecting! We don't have to try for number four; it is already on the way! I am almost four months along by my calculations!"

James grabbed his wife and hugged her ever so tightly. He questioned why she had not told him sooner. She told of what she believed to be the miscarriage and of how she wanted to be sure before she told him. She believed the baby would be born sometime in January. James was so happy! Lucy was so relieved. Number four was on its way and oh how they hoped it would be a boy. They now had two girls and one boy.

Another boy would even everything up in such a nice fashion.

Sometimes Lucy felt she and James had stretched their children out too far and maybe they would not be close with each other. She could only hope that when they became adults they would ignore the years between them and become the greatest of friends.

232

Chapter 22

October 6th, 1958, James and Lucille received a call they never wanted to receive. James's mother had passed away. She had last stayed with his brother Everett in Columbus, Ohio. Arrangements had to be made to bring her home to her family burial grounds. The service would be in Vinton at the funeral home. Lucy was so happy that she had told her mother-in-law of the birth of her 22nd grandchild. It hurt to know that she would never see him. Lucy knew her children and her husband were taking this death very hard. She could feel the pain of the loss deeply herself, but she knew she had to remain strong for all of them.

James was very worried for his wife. She did not need all of this stress with her pregnancy. He felt he had put too much upon her lately as it was. She often had to care for the store and she hated that. The duties she had at the church were very demanding. School had started and getting the children ready for school each day was a chore. Plus he had never gotten a hot water tank. Lucy was still boiling water to wash clothes in. She was boiling water for the whole family to bathe in. The containers used to boil the water were heavy and James knew no matter how many times he had ask her to wait for him to do these tasks, she had often done them herself.

Even fun things could be stressful. Just the previous night they had attended a 'Belling'. James's sisters had told him of how city folk had never heard of such a thing. He thought of how boring it must be to live in a city. A 'Belling' in this part of the country was held after a young couple got married. The newlyweds would never have an idea of just when this would happen, but they knew that it most surely would happen somewhere in their near future. The young couple would stock up on candy bars or ice-cream bars to be sure they would have treats for their guest after all of the craziness was finished.

All of the neighbors and friends would pick a night unbeknownst to the couple. They would wait until the newlyweds were in bed. The group would then gather all around the couple's house. They would be equipped with cow bells and all sorts of noise makers. The cowbells were of the most importance because of their noise. Once the group had screamed and rang their bells loud enough and long enough to wake up the dead, the couple would come to the door. At this time the young men were prepared to put the husband upon a log that they had brought with them. Once mounted, they would then parade the groom around the outside of house! This was always great fun for all.

James had asked Lucy if she felt well enough to attend this belling and she had said yes. He had started to worry of late because of her age and the pains she had been feeling. Although considered still young, thirty-two was much different than the early twenties in delivering a baby. He felt shame when he thought of how he had caused their life to go on as it always had.

Only a week ago, James had asked Lucy to do something he now feels he should not have done either. The old Sunday school bus picked a crazy time to break down this year. The church always had their Sunday school picnic in September. This year they were to go to Lake Hope. When the time arrived for the picnic, the church could not figure out how to get everyone to this lake that was some thirty miles away. James got the bright idea of putting the church bench seats in the back of his open ton and one-half Ford truck.

There were no seat beat rules in those days and doing things like this may have been somewhat commonplace. So a large group of adults and children loaded into the back of that truck and took off for their day of fun. James laughed as he watched all of the ladies adorning scarves. He waited patiently as each lady tied their pretty silk scarves around their chins. The guilt now was coming from the fact that James had agreed that Lucy could ride in the back with the others. He knows she had great fun, but now he feels that was silly on his part. Now, the death of his mother may be too much for his lovely wife.

Through the days of the funeral, Lucy survived quite nicely. She was hurt by the loss. She also hurt for her husband's big beautiful family and she hurt for her children. This matriarch of a lady had passed and left a very large legacy behind her.

On Monday after the family had dispensed back to their personal homes, James took Lucy to the doctor for a check-up. He was so relieved to find the pregnancy was still going just fine.

After dropping Lucy and the children back at the house, James had to catch up on his gas route. He felt he was behind after taking off the time to attend his mother's funeral. He knew his mind was not on his business of late with the passing of his precious mother and his wife being with child. This very day he realized that after he had traveled away from one of his customer's homes by the distance of about thirty miles that he had not made the correct change to the lady. He had to turn around and go back. He felt so badly about this. James was the most honest man anyone would ever know. He would have driven the thirty miles to correct an error if he had cheated the person out of three cents. That was just the kind of a man James George Dahl was!

Once he arrived back at the home and corrected his mistake, the family was most grateful. By now it was getting late into the afternoon and he had several stops to make before dark. So, he sped along his way. His next stop was to pick up money that a customer did not have upon his last delivery. The lady of the house had asked him to stop back by on any trip he had near her home. Trying to catch up with his work load, James pulled into this person's driveway and proceeded up the steps to the door. He knocked and knocked upon the door. He was about to believe there was no one at home. However, he thought he had heard something inside, so he knocked upon the door once more. He could see straight through the house because the front door had a large window in the center. Just as he was about to give up, he noticed a broom handle coming across the kitchen wall. He could now see the stove and noticed there was a pan boiling over. Obviously the lady of the house did not want to see him. Maybe she did not have the money today, because she was trying to remove the boiling food from the burner on the stove with a broom handle. James was surprised at first, but had to laugh at how she must have thought of him as intruding. James being James, he walked down the steps and got into his truck and left. This was his big laugh for the day. Most people would have been mad, but James found much humor in this lady's intuitiveness. His line of business had always given him many reasons to love it.

James had much time to think of his mother while he was on his gas route. He felt that his family was so blessed with the knowledge that she was now in Heaven. He almost felt jealous that she would get to see his father, his brother John, and his sister Gwen long before he would. His mother had suffered so much to where this was almost a relief. It was sad and hurtful to lose her, but he felt that his family should maybe rejoice because he knew his mother was finally completely happy. She was no longer attached to that bed that she had laid upon now for about four years. She could walk again! She could smile again! She could praise her God!

All through the week, James kept remembering the feeling he had been getting of late. He had felt very deeply that he was being called to be a preacher. He knew he should answer that calling. He had talked with his mother about this often while she was on her sick bed. She had told him of how she had never doubted that he would become a minister. She said that she had known that fact every since the days of his young youth. She reminded him of how he always preached to his siblings and friends. Now he wished he had made the decision before his mother's death. He had been very sure that preaching is what he was going to have to do no matter whether he wanted to or not. God expected it of him.

Just as before, doubts crossed James's mind. How could he spring his need to become a minister upon his lovely wife? She, of all people, would probably understand. She was, after all, a minister's daughter! But, how would they survive? Ministry did not pay well, especially if one pastored a small country church. James had a family of three children with one on the way. How could he provide for his family? Why would God expect him to do such a thing? Why had God lead him in the direction of business? His business was now very profitable. This business could give his family everything they needed and they could live with great comfort. All of these questions arose in James's mind. He kept questioning God. Little did he know that God had a plan? He had a plan that would protect James and his family. All James had to do was to put all of his faith and trust in Jesus! A passage in the Bible kept crossing James's mind. It went something like this:

"What would a man gain if he gained the whole world but lost his own soul?"

After much of going back and forth with God, James decided he would have to come out and tell the world about his need to become a minister. The first obstacle to cross was the telling of this news to his wife. The second would be to finish his education. He had been out of school for

238

so many years now. How would he even be able to study? Could he pass his examines, due to his father's untimely death and his being taken out of school before finishing? So many questions crossed the young man's mind.

On the day that James decided to tell his lovely wife, he was amazed at her acceptance of the fact. She told him that she already knew that he would someday become a minster and that he must follow God's wishes. She told him not to worry. She told of how if you worry, then that is a sign you do not have enough faith in God. If you have total faith in God, you cannot worry. James felt so much comfort in her words. Lucy never ceased to remind him in someway of all the reasons why he loved her so.

The next step would be to tell the church. He had to tell all of the members, family and friends of whom he had known all of his life. Would they believe him to have lost his mind? Would someone say what he had questioned himself, that maybe this was only grief talking because of the loss of his mother? He had learned this was not the case because he had been feeling the pressures to become a minister long before his mother's death.

James knew he could not delay with his calling, so the following Sunday he got up in front of his peers. As he began to speak, doubts and fears crossed through his mind. But, he continued with a steady voice. He said,

"Ladies and Gentleman, I need to make an announcement! The Lord above has called me to preach. I have been fighting this need for a very long time, but I cannot anymore. I'm scared, I'm worried but I must follow what God has planned for me!"

The crowd was silent for what James felt forever. He starred out into the congregation and into the eyes of all of those he loved so much. He looked at his sister Mabel who had stayed in their homeland the same as he. He saw big tears rolling down her cheeks. She stood up and said,

"Folks, there was never a doubt this would happen to my little brother! We, the family, all knew he was to be a minister, years ago!"

Before she was able to take her seat again, the whole crowd cheered. They were all happy for James. They all acted as though they were blessed to be in attendance upon this chosen morning.

After the services, everyone shook hands with James and gave him inspiring words of hope. He stayed afterwards so he could speak to the pastor. He had to ask the pastor just how one goes about becoming ordained. He knew he could ask many of these questions of his father-in-law, but he lived so very far away now. His in-laws had now moved to Florida for all winter months. They had purchased a home there in 1956. So on this morning of 1958, James was intent on listening to his hometown minister.

James found out what classes he would need to take from the Bible College in Circleville. He found out that he would be able to take correspondence courses. This would cause nothing to interfere with his business. He later told Lucy,

"See God has thought of everything. He knew I could not afford to stop and study. He is taking care of everything! God is GOOD!"

Lucy would laugh with him, hold his hand, and tell him of how blessed she felt to have him as her husband.

The next couple of years went by with all of the blessings one family could have. The business was thriving. A beautiful baby boy had been born into this wonderful household. His hair was of a platinum color, an almost white. He had the prettiest blue eyes and no one could keep their hands off of this little boy. There was only one major problem. The little lad had been born with Asthmatic Bronchitis! Before the beautiful child was one year old he had pneumonia three times. He had been hospitalized each time. The parent's heart would break when they watched their little boy cry from inside of a plastic tent full of ice. This was done to bring down his temperatures and this is what saved his life many times, but the feeling of helplessness on the parent's part was devastating.

By the time the fourth child of the James Dahl family turned eighteen months old, his sickness was not getting any better. Lucy and James had completed ever task the doctors had requested. The baby bed was in their bedroom. They had removed all fuzzy cloth items, such as blankets, carpets, and stuffed toys. Nothing could relieve the whizzing spells this little lad had. He would completely lose his breathing ability. This would cause many rushes to the hospital. Finally, the local doctors suggested the family move to a warmer climate. They told the family in all probability that their young one would outgrow much of this terrible condition. But to keep him safe until then, possibly a move would be the best thing. The doctors had suggested Arizona. James had told the doctors that was not even a possibility. Then the couple told the doctors about Reverend and Mrs. Herms living in Florida. It was decided that Florida was a warmer climate and maybe the child would develop better in those conditions.

The family was going to plan a move the following fall. Warmer weather in Ohio was okay for the child. Once the weather chilled, they planned to move. There was so much to be done. James must sell his gas route. There was a man who had seemed very interested in the route, but had shown concerns over the amount of work it caused a person. There was so much to do if a move would become possible.

Through the summer months, James studied for his ministry. The kind Mr. Jones did purchase the bottled gas business. The furniture store would need to be closed. The closeness of the store to their house would prevent anyone from purchasing the building. Besides, James and Lucy had no intention of selling anything. They felt their move was going to be temporary. The doctor had said their son should outgrow most of his condition. There was the service station to contend with and the few homes James had purchased to rent. Other than those things, plans were going along smoothly.

The service station had started out more or less as a competition James and the one and only other store owner of their small town had going. Jake Mills owned the general store with a gas pump. He also owned the feed store that was caddy cornered across the road from his store. For years there stood a large two story old brick building in the site directly across from the general store. No one seemed to know who owned this building and the property. Jake had tried many times to find the owner. James and he would laugh about it often when they would talk of who would own it first. Small towns seem to have these sorts of things going on. James, Jake and James's brother-in-law would often go down to the court house steps for sales of property in their little town. Though very close, these three big men would bid against each other. It was all in great fun.

Though it did not come about from an auction, James had won out on the property across the street from the general store. He rarely mentioned that he was a descendant of the founder of this very town. Actually, he never mentioned this fact. Most people did not know or did not remember that James's great, great something grandpa had built this town. Therefore it did not take too much of an effort for James to locate the rightful owners. They were distant relatives of his. This remained a joke to Jake and James for the rest of their lives. However, James built a service station on this spot. Not because he wanted a service station, but because he was already tied in with the refinery that furnished his LP gas. So, once the service station was complete, a brother of his brother-in-law managed the station. He was a good mechanic and did more repair work than selling gas. The move to Florida was not going to be hindered by the ownership of this business.

Chapter 23

It was a sad day for James and Lucille's oldest children on the day the family left for Florida. This meant they had to leave their lifetime friends and schoolmates. The oldest daughter cried most all of the way. Since the family was taking their furniture truck full of furniture, they had commissioned James's niece Carolyn and her new husband to drive the truck. When Lucille realized how distressed her daughter was she ask her if she would like to ride with her cousin. She lit up with that suggestion and at the next stop, she hurried back to ride with the two newlyweds. She worshiped her cousin; therefore Lucille knew she would have great fun back there. This decision should have been made from the beginning of this trip, but James and Lucille were trying to give Carolyn and her new husband a vacation or honeymoon of sorts.

Florida was beautiful, but was so remote. Many people were now retiring to these counties, but the one Lucille's parents lived in was a very back in the woods sort of place. The town had sand streets. There were small little houses up every one of them. Naturally, Lucille's mother had decorated her small home in the most beautiful of fashion. This lady could make an out house look good.

The Dahl family arrived in September 1960, just in time for the hurricane named Donna. The family had only been there a couple of weeks when this horrible storm hit the shores of Florida, USA. They had not found a place to live as of yet. All of their belongings were still on that truck. James had backed it up close enough to the garage so that he could plug in their freezer. The family always froze a full beef and a complete hog for the winter months. They could not afford to lose any of that meat.

When the hurricane struck, Reverend Herms refused the warnings to go to a shelter. This may have been wise because the shelter, for this town, was a very old private school building. The Reverend Herms and James prayed all night long while both repeating that God would watch over the family. When the force of this horrible hurricane hit with full blast, the radio went dead. This happened right at the time the announcer had said the storm was moving inland and the eye of the storm was coming straight towards the Herms home. All night the wind blew with severe force. It hit the house so hard that water was coming between the window panes as if each window was its' own water fall. Mrs. Herms spent hours trying to mop water out of her sunken living room floor. Reverend Herms opened the door opposite of the direction of the wind. He did this again when the calm time came as the eye passed over. This very educated man had done his homework. James and Lucille held their crying children close while they prayed.

After the storm on the following morning, there was flood water clear up to the front porch floor. The house across the street was no more.

Only a concrete slab lay there in the wake. The house behind the Herms home had a huge tree that had fallen right down through the middle of it. James's car had moved about seven feet and there was no electric anywhere. But the Herms home was standing steady without one spot of damage. On the second day the water had gone down enough for James to take the truck to the next town. Here there were businesses that had electric. James had asked someone if he could keep his freezer plugged into their place of business for a price.

A house that James and Lucille had looked at just the week before in hopes of renting it was now demolished. James knew it was God's will for them not to have gotten it. A week or so later the family did rent a home within blocks of Lucille's parents.

Winter and dampness came to Florida the same as anywhere else. It was just a warmer winter and a warmer dampness. Before the school year was over, the baby had already gone through the same asthmatic attacks that he had in Ohio. Lucille had enjoyed being close to her parents the months they lived in Florida, but as soon as school was out the family made the decision to move back to Ohio. The transition was softened by the fact that Lucille's parents were closing up their Florida home and heading back to Ohio for the summer. This was a practice they had started with their move to Florida. They would stay in Florida from October until May, and then they would stay in Ohio for the summer months.

James had never worked for anyone other than odd jobs in his entire life. He was a self made man. In Florida he had taken a salesman's position with a draw of only forty dollars a week. People were poor in this community so furniture did not sell well.

Being the entrepreneur that James was, he could not see that large furniture truck stay in his driveway and not make a profit. The wheels of that calculator brain started turning. He took the panels off his truck and built wooden side walls. He then went out and honestly leased orange groves. He then hired help and started hauling oranges.

Even with James's added income, there just was not enough to raise a family the size of his. This caused the Dahl family to use up much of their savings. Often James had felt the move was in vain, because he believed that the youngest son was outgrowing some of his condition. His attacks were further apart to date. Some may think that was because of Florida but it was just as the doctor had said. The baby was starting to outgrow his condition.

James felt they were moving back home in the nick of time. He knew he had to preach, but he had no idea what he would do other than preaching for a living. He was able to study a lot while living in Florida. He did not realize how he had filled all of the hours of his days without the workload at home. Work was massive on the farm as was the work he did with his Ohio company. Florida about drove him crazy because he had nothing to do! This was at least nothing to do in his way of thinking. So, he studied.

The trip home went very smoothly. The Dahl's felt that it was wonderful to be back in their old home again. That is all except their oldest daughter. She had not wanted to leave Ohio, now she had met friends in Florida and did not want to leave there. There didn't seem to be much one could do to please this teenager.

James found out almost immediately that the gentleman who had purchased his gas business was not in good health. He had purchased this business for his sons but to date none of them were able to help him. James went to visit the owner to see about buying back his business. James would buy back the business and work it as he always had but with the stipulation that if he ever wanted to sell it again he would allow the same family to purchase it. The owner agreed to these terms and James was so relieved.

It was not long before the family was back to complete normalcy. The only differences being, James had become somewhat afraid by now. The Florida money crunch had taken its toll on him. He refused to take the big chances he had once taken in business. Times were getting tougher and everyone was struggling to make a go of it. Many of James's customers could not pay on time. Many could not pay at all. There was no contract between James and his customers, only faith and someone's word. James preferred it that way.

The younger sister Bella, and James and Lucille's daughter Hannah, got together one weekend and decided they were going to collect from everyone who owed James money. They bought stickers that said things like 'PAST DUE' and so on. They started laughing more than collecting when they found that people owed bills for ten or fifteen years. Someone owed James for pigs he had sold in 1944. Just at the time all of the bills were typed up and spread all over the kitchen table, James came in from his route. He started picking up each and every bill and stacked them neatly to one side. He was standing tall with that frame of an ox. The ladies were seated. He said in a stern voice,

"Girls, I will not allow these to be mailed! If these friends and neighbors of mine could pay their bills, then they would pay their bills. This whole community is full of good honest God loving people and I will not add stress to their lives. Every one of these people has told me they will pay me when they can."

Bella shook her head. Lucille and her daughter hung theirs. They all knew James very well and they knew what he was going to say next. He said,

"God has and always will provide for us. He has never let us down and I know He is not about to let us down now. We have to live by faith. He said He would never allow more to come over us than we can bear. He also said he would take care of His children."

With that outburst, James headed out the door to do his chores. Bella walked over to the corner, picked up a trash can and slid all of their hard work off of the table into it. She patted Lucille on the back as she passed her chair and said,

"Oh, yea of little faith!"

In a few days, Bella went home to her family with a new kind of love for her brother. She always knew he was special but maybe forgot just how much along the way. This man was the most honest, loving man she would ever know. She wondered if her father was that way too. She could not remember her father, but knew her brother James had to get all of that kindness from somewhere. Oh, all of the siblings and their mother were of the most kind, but James, now he was hard to explain. The only thing she could think of was that he was probably more like God than anyone you could ever meet. He lived by faith. He lived for God. He lived his life walking the straight and the narrow. He had a deadly fear of ever doing anything to displease his Heavenly Father. A better man had never walked this earth.

During the following months, James studied every minute he could. In August he was to take his examines. To be ordained he must make a higher grade. He was worried, but knew God had bigger plans for him, therefore he knew he would pass the tests. When the time came, he did just that. He passed! And with flying colors! Now he must sit back and wait for God's new direction.

Chapter 24

Before long, the now Reverend James George Dahl was pastoring a church of his very own. It was a small little church that was about twenty miles from his home, but it was his church. His very own church! James and Lucille laughed at how one could not say anything about any of the members of this church because it seemed everyone was related.

One advantage this small church had over many others in the community was that this church was the home church of a group of professional singers. They traveled all of the time around the country on their bus, but on those Sunday's that these groups were home at their own church were heavenly. James loved their music so very much.

James pastored this church for eight years. During this time, he kept his businesses. The payment that the church put aside for their pastor was placed directly back into the offering plate by the Reverend James Dahl.

Young couples would come to the furniture store to look at furniture. James would joke with them and say,

"I am a minister. I will make you a good deal on a house full of furniture and marry you too boot! Then I will sell you a kitchen stove and be your gas man. See how lucky you are for stopping at this one stop shop!"

He would then throw his head back and roar with laughter. This would always cause much fun and laughter to anyone who came in contact with this wonderful man. He had other sayings that had become well known as well. One was,

"That item is $300.00 to anyone else, but to you my friend it will be $299.99."

Everyone loved James George Dahl. The church women and any woman who knew him loved what they called his bear hugs. He was such a large man and so very charming that everyone felt safe in his loving arms. He had no fear of what anyone might say badly about him. Everyone felt his closeness to God and no one ever did talk badly about him. No one found anything bad that they could say about him. He lived his life above reproach. His way of living his life and this kind of personality made everything alright.

On Saturdays during the weekly family shopping trips to Gallipolis, James would speak with everyone. He was well known by doctors, attorneys, laymen and even the one and only town prostitute. Others were afraid to speak to this woman in public. Not James, he was always very kind. He would invite her to church. He would tell her he was praying for her. He would take her hands in his and tell her if she ever wanted to get right with God to please let him know. He would be there to pray for her at any time.

This great big heart did so many wonderful things. During these times the only sort of telephone lines the community had, was party lines. James picked up the phone one day to make a call and overheard a neighbor, who was a superintendent of a construction company. He was telling someone he needed a flagman for his road crew. Being not a nosy person, James spoke up. He may have felt more comfortable in doing so since this gentleman was married to his first cousin but more than likely would have felt the need out weighed any rudeness in this jester. He spoke up by saying,

"Johnny, I'm sorry to butt in, but I have the most perfect person for that job."

A wonderful family had moved up the street from the Dahl's. They had moved to Ohio from Kentucky or West Virginia. James was not sure which state. Anyway, the father had looked *unsuccessfully* for a position in the local community. James knew these people from the time they had lived in a smaller house out in the country. He had delivered gas to them. Both the husband and the wife were most nice. The lady always offered James something wonderful to eat when he made his delivery. Now they had purchased a house in the small town and the man needed a job desperately. Luckily, the neighbor hired the friendly man and this family stayed on in the community to become life time friends.

Deeds like these were very common for James George Dahl. One time, however, this great big heart got him into deep, deep trouble. Financing furniture purchases had become straining for James. Someone told him to run his customers through a finance company. That way he would receive his money up front and the people would make their payments to the finance company. This was working just great until the day he met the soon to wed couple by the name of Tingess.

The young couple stopped by the furniture store and looked around for a good while. James ran his speech by the couple of how he could marry them and sell them their first house full of furniture. The couple loved this idea. They chose the best of furniture. They did not see a bedroom suit that they liked, so James made arrangements with them to take them to the wholesale house in Charleston, West Virginia the following week. There they could pick out one that they did like.

The couple took James up on the wedding ceremony throw in. The following month they brought a group of friends and family to the furniture store where the wedding was held. James was proud of himself. He kept telling Lucille of how he started this wonderful couple out in life. He said he was able to tell them all about Jesus as well and hoped they would attend his church before long.

Before delivering the furniture, James took the young couple to Gallipolis where they had to go to the finance company to sign the papers for financing. Once they arrived and spoke with the good loan manager, things became depressing for the young couple. James found that this couple did not have enough credit to buy the furniture they had chosen. The loan officer said,

"Mr. Tingess, you and your wife will need a co-signer if you wish to have a loan."
James listened as the couple discussed of how they knew no one who could possibly sign for them. Being the romantic that he was, caught up in the minute and the pride that he had joined these two in Holy Matrimony; James reached across the desk, picked up the papers and signed them. The

loan officer, who was also a friend, gave James the most shocked look as he said,

"James, I wish you had not done that. The seller should not be the co-signer."

James laughed and said,

"I married this couple. They're sweet people and someone has to give them a good start in life."

Well, that good start in life ended up with only a couple of payments paid. Then it was as if the couple had fallen off the planet. When the loan company and James tried to locate this couple, they had moved the furniture from the delivery house. The sheriffs department found they had left the state. The lawyers, judges and the loan officer informed James that they could not go out of the state to collect on this debt. James was devastated. He had to pay for the furniture, now twice. Only this time it was at the retail value and with added interest! James, always finding something good in every situation felt God must have had a reason. The reason may have been if for nothing else but to humble him. For the rest of the days, James whom the loan officer and other friends had called 'Easy Money' was now branded by the name of 'Mr. Tingess'. He would walk into a bank or doctor's office and someone would holler,

"Hello Mr. Tingess, how are you?"

James would always laugh with the hackler and count his many blessing for having so many wonderful friends. He could always rest assured that when he arrived at his old friend army doctors office he would be greeted by the talking miner bird that always said very correctly,

"Hello, Mr. Dahl!"

He somehow never thought that would be something he would look forward to until after the Mr. Tingess ordeal.

As years went by, family reunions, camp meetings, tent meetings, rivals, the death of many dear friends and the arrival of many new ones, James and Lucille had a very happy life. The children grew up and got married. The oldest daughter got a divorce and struggled to take care of her children. James and Lucille sold their much loved home to move close to her to help while she worked on her job and her future.

The church they had remarked about all members being relatives had now become relatives of theirs. Their oldest son had married one of those gospel singers. James loved to hear her beautiful voice and was so very proud of his daughter-in-law. Lucille's brother Lewis had divorced after sixteen years of marriage. He spent a lot of time with his sister Lucille. Before the term of pastoring James's church was up, he too had met a lady at this church and married her. She was a distant cousin of the daughter-in-law singer. James always had to laugh about that. He would often say it was one of those, 'I'm my own grandpa' scenarios.

After leaving this church, James built a large stage upon his farm. Years after selling his gas route the second time to the same family who had purchased it years ago, James and Lucille had moved back to the countryside. He had taken the position of associate pastor at his home church. He had opened another furniture store in a neighboring town and the couple was living in and remodeling James's childhood home. Each summer James would have a songfest on the Dahl hilltop. The professional singers and their groups would pull their large buses into the yard and put on an all day show at the old Dahl farm. The family friends who owned the local funeral home would furnish chairs and tents. The whole community would attend. The singing groups would sing for hours. Then everyone would have a potluck meal in the yard. This was a very special day for James.

James later built a new home for his bride. This is what he would always call Lucille. The youngest son, his wife and two children would be moving into the old farm house. Once again it needed remodeled and the young couple took on this great task. James and Lucille built their new home in the very place where the long red chicken houses stood during James's youth. In the back yard, James who was handy with a saw, nail and hammer, built another building. He built a shelter house that had many tables. He built a fire pit and everything that a shelter house may need. He chose to do this for many reasons. One reason was so he could bring all of his family reunions to the old home place. All members, from all sides of his family, remembered this beautiful old place as magical. The new shelter house would be used for all reunions and many church functions. This was an asset to the property.

In his sixties James found that he had a terrible condition. He had cancer. His little sister Edith had died recently of the horrible disease. The loss of this loving sister had cut James very deeply. His baby sister Bella hopefully had caught the same disease in time and had a breast removed. Now, he was third on the list to get this disease. The good doctors requested that he have a massive operation. They were going to remove a large amount of his intestines.

Lucille and her adult children waited the many hours of the operation. They had this operation completed once, only to have to redo the same procedure hours later. One daughter-in-law and one cousin, being nurses who worked for that same hospital, kept the family more informed. They would stop by while on their shifts to console the worried family. Even with all of their professionalism, one could see they were worried too. The final result was that the doctors had to remove about three feet of James's intestine. He would have to wear a bag upon his side for the rest of his days.

Lucy could not help but remember the days when her family was so concerned about her wanting to date Mr. James Dahl. Now, this very night, the Herm's family was each and everyone snuggled close together in that waiting room. They were all praying and waiting for what they hoped to be good news about their precious James. Reverend Herms had brought along lots of strong coffee for the group. Lucille's mother had made a wonderful trail mix to comfort each family member through their long hours of waiting. Everyone loved James so very much. After much praying and the Good Lord blessing this family, James awakened and the recovery and healing were almost instant. God's hands blessed him.

Reality was sitting in for this couple as they arrived home from the hospital. James had always been self employed. This meant he did not have insurance. He had a little death insurance through the ministry, but nothing for hospital bills. This stressed Lucille to the point that she picked up her phone once more and ask the prayer chain to please pray that she and James could somehow find means to pay this massive hospital bill. James, on the other hand, would take his wife into his arms and say,

"Honey, God has always been good to us, He will provide. You know He will provide!"
Lucy would watch James with her all knowing eyes. She knew he was worried sick. She would then say to him,

"Why worry Darling, when you can pray?"
This seemed to be her motto. Now if she could just practice what she preached.

Word passes very fast in small communities. Within a week, a group of cars pulled into the Dahl driveway. Many friends and loved ones had been to visit and there to pray with James, but never had there been this many at one time. James and Lucille watched out of the window in amazement. James said,

"Maybe they are bringing the church service to us since they know I have not been able to attend."

The knock came at the door. Lucy rushed to the door to answer. There stood Brother Jones with a group of other church members. A large group of neighbors were behind them. Lucy stood there with her mouth wide open. Brother Jones asked if they could please come in. Lucy, in her amazement, said,

"Of course, please do come in! I will make some coffee."
Brother Jones said,

"Wait a minute Lucille. We have something very important to tell James and we would like for you to be present."

Lucy fell to a chair. Brother Jones went over to the large picture window and tapped on it. Shortly thereafter a group of young men from the church marched into the house. They were each carrying a five gallon galvanized bucket. Each young man placed a bucket in front of James's recliner where he was resting. Lucy gasped as she looked down into the buckets. Each bucket was filled completely full of money. She said,

"What is this?"

Brother Jones spoke again,

"James, you have been our friend, our minister, our family and a dear loved one to all of us for years and years. You have always been there in anyone's time of need. We have survived with the help of your care. Shoot, I think everyone of us is running on your prayers. For all of these years you delivered gas to over six hundred of us customers. You never refused to keep us warm. You never hesitated to furnish our homes with the needed element to cook our food. Many times we did not have enough money to pay you; yet you cared for each and every one of us enough to see that we were provided for. Now it is our turn to help you, our dear servant of God. Now it is our turn!"

James rose from under his blanket and put his arms around his dear old friend. By now the rooms full of people had their eyes filled with tears. Someone said,

"We hope there is enough here to pay your hospital bill."

Through tear filled eyes, James said,

"You know there is! God *DOES* provide our needs!"

Chapter 25

February 06, 1992 the community held a large celebration for James and Lucille's fiftieth wedding anniversary. They renewed their vows in a church ceremony. This was Lucille's choice because when they married the first time they had held their ceremony in the family living room. The reception had so many people in attendance to where it had to be held in the school gymnasium.

Lucy was fortunate in the fact that her father and mother were still around to enjoy this event. The good Reverend Herms was there to give his daughter to James a second time. All of the family came to enjoy this special occasion. Both of their sons lived on the farm. The oldest daughter and her husband flew in from Florida. The other daughter and her husband came in from Columbus, Ohio. By now James and Lucille were the proud grandparents of six grandchildren, and several step grandchildren. They were even great grandparents at this time.

James's sister, Mabel, who had been the only sibling that remained in the county of their birth, had been the postmaster there for many years. Now retired, the doctors had found she had bone cancer and did not give her long to live. Two years earlier, James had lost his wonderful sister

Elizabeth to cancer. Just a couple of years before that, he had lost his brother Everett to brain cancer.

During the mid 1990's, James had lost most of his siblings. They were dying one every two years. There were only four of them left at this date. The sadness this brought James was changing him. Luckily, his cancer had never come back. He had survived ten years and was most surely past the danger times. He had, however been treated for two major heart attacks. He had been in the hospital many times with this condition. He was the only member of his family to have any heart trouble. Of course he was the largest of all members and he knew, by today's standards, he did not eat properly. He could not understand the cancers in his family. His sister Mabel had a daughter who had almost died of cancer at her young age. Only prayers had saved her life. His sister Edith, who had lost her life much earlier to the same illness, had also lost a twenty-nine year old son to the horrible disease. The family now believed if the proper diagnose had been given way back when their father passed, that it would have more than likely been brain cancer. That must surely be where this horrible disease came from.

James tried to think of more cheerful things. His oldest grandson was getting married. The lad's younger sister had beaten him to the punch and married a few years before. She had lived in the south the same as her mother and brother but had since gotten a divorce. She and her baby had then moved back to be with James and Lucille. The divorce had saddened James. He had married the couple in his very own church and wished for no one's marriage to go astray. He did, however, enjoy every minute he could spend with his beloved great granddaughter. His granddaughter had even given him permission to give the child her middle name. He would burst with pride when he was with this wonderful child.

James felt very, very blessed in so many ways. His two sons lived on each side of him. He was lucky in that respect. Both sons were tall. His youngest son had grown up to be a large, strong and healthy man the same as his father. He and his lovely wife had two children, a boy and a girl. These two were both in High School at this time and James was enjoying them growing up. He loved the fact that they popped in and out of his door whenever they wished. The granddaughters and the great granddaughter knew they had grandpa wrapped around their little fingers. James would completely melt when any one of them was around.

The oldest grandson was having a very large church wedding in a southern state. This was to be a beautiful Catholic wedding and James had been ask to speak. He was to have a part in the wedding along with the Priest. James felt so honored that his grandson would wish him to do such a thing.

The Dahl's traveled to this state for the weekend wedding and all was well with this beautiful family. What a wonderful time was had by all. James could not help but blow up with pride when he hugged his pretty, petite granddaughter-in-law to be. The family was growing fast at this point. James would look around at the large crowd and jokingly ask,

"Lucille, did we cause all of this?"

The nineties were moving fast. On one occasion, James and Lucille visited their daughter in Florida. They rode down with their youngest son and his family in their luxury van. This was their first trip to Florida since the day they had moved there many years ago. Their daughter had a beautiful home on the beach. James would spend long hours of this visit meditating and looking out over the water. He told his family that he did not feel he had long left upon this old earth. He pointed out to everyone that if the ocean and the surrounds were that beautiful, then imagine at how beautiful Heaven must be.

Back on the home front, James continued to preach the message. He would preach and halfway sing his way through most sermons. His sermons were all so very moving. Everyone knew when they listened to this minister that they were hearing from someone who lived that very life. He was one who definitely practiced everything he preached. He was the same on Monday as he would be on Sunday. This man lived the most wonderful wholesome and honorable life. He would start preaching while many times quoting his text without even opening his Bible. He would get excited and hold his Bible up high above his head. It would sound as if he was reading every line written, however there were often times that the Bible may even be upside down. James had a beautiful singing voice and he would often break into a half preach and a half song performance such as,

"All my sins are washed away! They've been washed by the blood of the lamb!"

James could not play the trumpet anymore because he needed the suction of having natural teeth. Several years ago he had been given false teeth. He missed his much loved trumpet and coronet. He had taken up the hobby more recently of playing his harmonica. He had always been a music lover. During the days when this big man loaded and unloaded that old stocker furnace of their first home, he could be heard singing. He often sung to Lucille that old song,

"You Are My Sunshine."

Each of his girls and the granddaughters heard this song sung to them many times throughout their lives. Never once did he fail to sing to his bride. He never failed to tell her how very much he loved her. This was the same for all of his children. Not a visit or a phone call would go by that they were not told of how much he loved them.

February 1996 came with James in the hospital. His daughter called from Florida and they talked a good while. He told her he did not want the family circle to be broken in Heaven and he hoped she was attending church somewhere. This was always the jest of his conversations with his children. He prayed everyday that each and every one of his children would go to Heaven. As fate would have it, he was placed in a room with another man. This man turned out to be one of his very favorite cousins. Though James was sick from still another heart attack, his cousin was there because of his kidneys. The nurses had to keep reminding the two that they were sick. When that did not work and they could be heard down the hall with their loud laughter, a nurse would stick her head in around the door long enough to say,

"Hey fellows, there are sick people on this floor."

All of the great fun of this hospital visit came to an end. As did the lack of realization that James was very, very sick. His heart attacks had damaged a very large percentage of his heart. It was so damaged to where no procedure like he had had before would do any good. It was too damaged for an operation of any kind. It would not help.

On a weekend in May, the head pastor of the church went on a much needed vacation. James was to care for both the morning and the evening services. Sunday morning came with the normal routines. While James and Lucille were getting dressed for church, Lucille would be preparing fried chicken or maybe baking a pie for their after church Sunday meal. Sunday meals were always the highlight of the week for all of these church going people. Sunday services, Sunday meal, then afternoon visits and rest. James would listen to gospel singers and maybe a minister or two on the T.V. This Sunday morning, James told Lucille he was not feeling so well.

They went to church, James preached the morning service. They had their meal and James went in to lie down. He told Lucille he did not feel well, at all. After sleeping away a big part of the afternoon, James started to get ready for the evening service. Lucille became worried at the way he looked and at how he told her he felt. She asked him to please cancel the trip to church and go to the hospital instead. James would have none of that. He said,

"No, I want to go to church."

Lucille did not know how to drive a car, therefore she got in on the passengers side for the two mile trip to the country church. Once they arrived at the church and the service began, James acted his normal self. He did, however, ask to be anointed with oil. This was a procedure rarely used in any church in these times. It was a procedure where one was to rub oil or ointment on a part of a person's body, usually the head or feet, as part of a religious ceremony. According to the Bible, this was a healing ritual. James knew his Bible well. If he wished to have this anointment, then it shall be done. Everyone prayed with their beloved leader.

James got up from his anointment having a glow over his face. He walked up to the pulpit and delivered his sermon. He stopped in the middle of the sermon and said,

"I am going to do something tonight that even my wife does not know I am doing."
Having everyone's curiosity up, he reached into his pocket and pulled out his harmonica. He started playing this small musical instrument to an old Christian song. The crowd believed the music sounded as if an angel were playing. He played a couple of songs, and then he ended his performance with 'Amazing Grace'. He would stop playing long enough to say,

"How sweet the sound."
The crowd cheered. Many had tears flowing down their faces. Before James stepped off the podium, he told all of his friends and neighbors that he loved them. This might have not been that unusual but tonight he sounded so final. He said,

"I love you all. God loves you. I plan on going to Heaven and someday I want you all to join me there. Please be ready to go when your time comes."

269

Then he kicked up a heel into the air as he often did and quoted some old words out of an old song,

"Won't it be wonderful there?"

He hugged all of his friends, but did not linger for conversation as he often did after these services. He and Lucy headed home. Not much was said on the short trip home. He did seem to be driving more irately than usual.

Once the couple arrived home, Lucy disappeared into another room to change her clothing. James took off his suit jacket and landed himself down into his recliner. All of a sudden, he hollered for Lucille to come to the living room to listen to his heart. She came running and did just that. As she listened, she knew they were in big trouble. His heart beat seemed to have gone. Just gone away! All she could hear was a sound that sounded like a waterfall gushing down over its' walls. She said,

"Oh My Honey! You are in trouble!"

She ran to the phone and called 911. Then she ran to the front door and screamed for help. The youngest son's house was only yards away.

Lucy ran back to her husband. James tried to stand up to hug his wife. He said,

"This is it Lucy, I will see you in Heaven! I love y---------!"

He did not get all of the 'you' out, as he crumbled to the floor. He fell with one leg buckling up under his body. Everyone came running. His large eighteen year old grandson had taken CPR in school and he began working furiously with his grandfather. After what seemed an eternity, the ambulance arrived. They stuck huge needles directly into his heart. They finally loaded him and Lucille into the ambulance and rushed to the hospital. The whole family arrived shortly after the ambulance. At about 1:00am the doctor walked in to tell the family that the Reverend James George Dahl had taken his last breath. Lucy knew he had died on their living room floor and the workers had only continued their services because her grandson had started CPR.

The next few days were a haze for Lucille. The family, friends and food kept coming. Her oldest son was in the shelter house with the radio on. It was tuned to a station where the announcer was one of James's church members from the church he had pastored for so many years. The announcer's heart was breaking. Between each song this announcer would say,

"We lost a great man today. We lost the best friend I will ever have. We lost a man who walked closer to God than any I have ever known or of any I will ever know. We lost a man of all men."

Lucille could hear her children tell others that they were worried about their lives now. Who was going to pray for them? Whose prayers were going to keep them safe? She watched as her oldest daughter excused herself away from the massive amount of people all over the living room and kitchen while she retreated to a bathroom. Her oldest daughter-in-law went in to check on her after she had been gone so long. Lucille walked by the door to hear them both crying uncontrollably. She heard her daughter say,

"I feel like one of those very tall buildings that have an extra large block in the corner. The block that tells the dates this building was built and so on. I feel like someone has jerked that huge block right out from under me and I am now wobbling."

Lucille also listened to her youngest daughter-in-law when she said, through her tears, that she wanted to buy Pop some warm socks. She told of how his feet were always cold. She overheard a daughter ask her non-believing husband if he now believed in God. She heard him reply,

"I believe in your Father honey, I will always believe in your Dad!"

Then she heard her oldest granddaughter as she stood by his casket say,

"He doesn't smell like grandpa!"

This was after she had leaned over to kiss her grandfather. She heard later that this same granddaughter had taken a bottle of his 'Old Spice' and put a few drops under his lapel. She heard her daughters talking about how they were, at separate times, over their father crying and both claimed to have heard him say,

"I'm not in here. You know that!"

Both felt he was more or less chewing them out for so little faith. They knew he had always said that the dead body was but a shell. The soul of a Christian is in Heaven! She wondered if they just imagined this; but found it very strange that they would both have the same story. She did know both of them had stopped crying at that point. Later she had gone into her bedroom for something where she found her six year old great granddaughter standing in a darkened corner while holding her grandfather's glasses in her little hands. The little girl had such a hurt look on her porcelain like pretty face as she starred into space. Then she overheard her oldest grandson cry and say,

272

"He will never know my baby!"

The grandson's wife was unable to come because their first child was due at any minute now. Lucy was falling apart, but she knew her family was feeling every drop of that pain as well. She wished she could be strong for her children.

Visiting hours at the funeral home were extended because people kept coming in. They were arriving from miles and miles around. Foreseeing this, the funeral director had already made arrangement for an extra viewing at the church for one hour before the service. This did not help the situation this evening. At eleven o'clock, Lucille was told that there were still people stretched around a full city block awaiting their turn to come in to pay their respects to their beloved James.

At the funeral people had to line up against the walls. Extra chairs were placed up and down the aisles. There was an ocean of people standing outside and loud speakers were placed so that they could hear the service. The singer, his daughter-in-law, sang his favorite song, 'God Walks The Dark Hills'. She could have never made it through this because of her deep love for her father-in-law had it not been for her professionalism.

The service was beautiful. Sobs and cries were coming from everywhere. James's many nieces and nephews passed by him while many leaned down to kiss their wonderful uncle. Some stood for long periods of time while their whole bodies shook with the tears that were flowing down their faces. A mountain could have been built with the love that was pouring out for this wonderful man this day.

As the crowd passed by, while hugging Lucille and the others on their way out of the church, Lucille's body was trembling. What was she to do without her wonderful husband? Everyone will go home and she will be left all alone. Her children all took their needed time to say goodbye to their father and grandfather. Each was very much aware of the huge loss they had just endured. Not one of them understood how they could go on without this master of his family. Not one of them was sure of their life without this strong man to guide them. For James's last two siblings, Bella and Dale Henderson, they had walked through this valley of death so many times with their family. They could only think of the reunion the large group must be having in Heaven without them.

Finally everyone was in their cars and headed for the cemetery. The white hearse was used for this very special man. Lucille and her children watched as the white hearse carried their ever so dear husband, father and grandfather to his resting place. The family and friends who followed were grieving themselves. The hearse was white, but the day was a very black, black day for so many hundreds of these people. How could any one man mean so very much to so many people? This loving group must now put their friend, their mentor, their loved one and this bigger than life kind of man into the cold, cold ground. Everyone felt if he could die, what could happen to them. Without him who could one go to for comfort? Who could one go to for advice or for a prayer? Who could one go to for a laugh, a song or just a big bear hug? This bright May day had turned into one of the saddest days for the good people of Gallia County.

Time passed and pain lessoned. Nothing was ever the same after this great loss. Lucille finally adjusted to living alone. She had not been without her wonderful husband since that day when she was only a teen. The adjustment was so hard for her. But she proved to be a very strong woman. Her faith in God and her determination to see her beloved husband once again kept her going. At seventy years old, Lucille took her drivers license test and she passed. Although a very strong woman, with the loss of her husband she would have believed that to have been her biggest loss. Fate was not through with this lovely lady yet. Lucille lived to see her parents and her brother Lewis pass on. She had thought James died young at seventy-four, but Lewis had died at seventy-two. Then the *worst tragedies* of them all that ripped her heart right out and made her life to never be normal in anyway again was when she lost a granddaughter in 1998, then a great grandson in 2009. These children lived on each side of her and she had cared for them most every day. Both were lost to horrible accidents. Without her faith in God, her family and her church she would have never been able to carry one.

Lucille talks to James, you know. She told of how he comes and visits her at times. She believes she can watch him while he basks in Heaven's glory. She knows that she never has to question where her loving husband is. She knows!

The memories that this beautiful lady has of this love story, no one could ever write. James has been gone now for many years but Lucy still feels his presence. She has the memories of her tall, strong, handsome husband. She can feel his big arms around her. He held her close for over fifty years. Lucille tells her children that one of these days she will go to bed and wake up the next morning in Heaven with James. She tells of how James will be standing there with his big arms wide open when God calls his daughter home.

Everyone who knew this couple will know it too. When God says to that pretty little blonde,

"Welcome home Lucille Herms Dahl! A job well done, come and be with your wonderful husband and join him in our 'Holy Choir' at this beautiful place that we call Heaven."

"You will forever be in our hearts."